MORE!

Tammie Rothermel

ISBN 978-1-0980-8852-1 (paperback)
ISBN 978-1-0980-8853-8 (digital)

Stonehome Publishing, Inc.
P.O. Box 17899
Fountain Hills, AZ 85269

To God in thanksgiving for His Holy Spirit
who inspired me and kept me moving forward
with positive reinforcement.
To my loving husband, Jerry,
for all his encouragement and understanding.

Extraordinary transformation steals in on the back of small, inconsequential moments.

CHAPTER 1

★

Moments

Nestled in a wide hollow within the virgin woods of the Oley Valley, a pristine white clapboard farmhouse with forest-green shutters sat insulated from the world. A herringbone redbrick drive curved through the thickets down to the seven-acre farmstead called *Creekside*. White-board paddock fencing cordoned off the property from the bluestone cindered lane out front. Amid these rolling hills, covered bridges, and lush woodlands, steadfast German traditions tempered every aspect of life.

Richard Moore, a precious stones merchant originally from England, and Fran, an idealistic American graduate of political science, found the rural hills of Pennsylvania a perfect compromise in which to raise their daughter. From the beginning, they raised Nicole to be a self-thinker—with beliefs grounded in God and traditional Dutch values. They taught Nicole to examine the facts and to educate herself on her positions. Nightly they served up healthy discussions of politics, religion, or ethics along with dinner. In those spirited debates, her parents forged her core beliefs. But sometimes Nicole's hot little temper, her flair for the melodramatic, or her innate trusting naiveté trumped their lessons in common sense and logic.

Saturday, March 7, 1964, offered nothing special, just the portend of a bountiful spring bursting through the winter-dry brush, surrounding the man-made lake where Nicole often took up sanctuary. An ordinary teen, giddy one moment, absorbed to the hilt the

5

next, Nicole often rode her horse, Thunder, down to the lake with Beau, her golden retriever, in tow. There she pondered life, daring to dream of turning her Sunday morning church vocals and high school musicals and choir experience into a singing career. Often she blessed the shimmering water and sentinel forest with her crystal voice.

That morning vacillated between crisp sunshine and threats of rain from steel-blue clouds. The stiff wind that changed the face of the sky tangled Nicole's long ebony hair and whistled through the empty tree limbs, obscuring the sounds of a car door slamming and a man tromping through the brittle weeds. He wore dark glasses and a hat with lures on it, pulled low on his forehead, to the top of his shades. Collar-length brown hair hung out from underneath the hat. He kept his focus down, as he picked his way toward the lake.

Sensing impending danger, Beau grew anxious with the first sounds of the intruder. Thunder pawed and neighed. Immersed in thought, Nicole dismissed their warnings. As the stranger neared, Beau accelerated his nervous pacing. His clatter masked the crack of the grass behind her. Finally standing up to quell her restless troops, she came face-to-face with the man. They startled each other. From low in his throat, Beau growled a warning. Nicole's heart pounded. She didn't shush Beau; she made the stranger disclose his intentions first.

"Oh, sorry, miss. I-I didn't mean to scare you." Obviously flustered, the man picked up the rod and tackle he dropped in the commotion. "I'm just here to do a spot of fishing. Mind if I take up a seat over there?" He gestured to a place about a hundred feet away.

"No, of course not," Nicole lied. She minded. This was her lake, and she wasn't used to sharing. Returning to her spot, Nicole tried to recapture her reverie of the day, but *he* continued to creep into her focus. Intense curiosity filled her bright turquoise eyes. She wondered about him.

Still intent on the interloper, Beau warily circled him, sniffing the air. No doubt the golden's actions unnerved the man. Unwrapping a roll from his tackle box, the stranger offered peace.

Seizing the opportunity of her dog's rude behavior, Nicole advanced her investigation. "Beau, leave the man alone. He's here to fish. Come on." She tugged on his collar, but Beau strained against her, sniffing the offering. "No. That's not polite!"

"Really. He's okay. Is he friendly? I haven't been 'round a dog in so long. Can he stay, then?" An English accent crept out as the stranger spoke.

"You're British? Your accent sounds similar to my father's. He's a Brit. Well, he was a Brit. I mean, he still sounds British…"

"Yeah? I'm here on business and needed a bit of time on my own. What about you?"

"Oh, we live down the road a mile or so. By the way, I'm Nicole Moore." The sixteen-year-old stuck out her hand.

"Oh, I'm a… G-G-Gordon," he lied, but what did it matter? Innocently enough, the interloper invited Nicole to sit. Over conversation, he shyly removed his hat and glasses, exposing his soft, warm brown eyes and angular thin face. Nicole guessed him to be in his early twenties. Her mind calculated the age difference. Summoning all the feminine wiles available to her, she monitored her speech and mannerisms to bridge the age chasm.

Each passing moment deepened Nicole's intrigue and mounting infatuation with the stranger. The attentions of an "older man," particularly one with an accent, easily turned her adolescent head. After the British invasion of the Merseymen, the Beatles, and the Stones, accents—anything from across the Pond—sent giggly girls into a delirium. However, something about Gordon seemed familiar. But making a determination about him eluded Nicole, since he intentionally avoided all her personal questions.

As much as Gordon set Nicole's head spinning, this quick, attractive "bird" with raven hair catching on her pert little breasts and mesmerizing turquoise eyes, who hadn't recognized him as one of the Merseymen, arrested his attention. Had he actually managed to snag the attention of such a beauty, without her swooning at his feet because he happened to be Grant Henderson, lead guitarist of the internationally celebrated rock group? Had he found the one bird in the whole world who fancied him for himself, not his fame? Definitely, this engaging chick ignited his interest.

And didn't he deserve it? He had survived the arduous, hammer-and-tong six-year claw to the top of the music heap. And once on top, for these long years, he conformed to the pressurized life inside the whirlwind of fame. Celebrity wasn't all adulation: different dollies nightly in the sack, and great, obscene gobs of money. Intense fame, such as the Merseymen had mined, exacted a price. It held them hostage inside hotel rooms—endless, faceless, same cities where nothing changed other than the names at the bottom of the ashtrays—sweltering rooms full of glaring, hot lights teemed with brash reporters who asked the same insipid questions over and over, then expected fresh, alive answers. And where your family of bandmates, managers, and roadies never went away and were always in your face day after day, hour after hour, for months on end, and where no one outside that circle could be trusted.

Played out and spent after the grueling years, Grant Henderson had cracked, abandoning his bandmates in Philadelphia. Driving into the countryside, he wanted to breathe the breath of freedom. He never expected—never wanted—an entanglement. But that's exactly what he found in that small, inconsequential moment when he met Nicole Moore, and she didn't recognize him.

The interloper had penetrated the sanctity of the Moores' sheltered existence.

CHAPTER 2

★

Decisions

Grant Henderson returned to the Merseymen in time for their concert in Philadelphia that night. But not before securing a promise from Nicole to meet him back at the lake for another rendezvous the following day.

As Nicole's image faded from his rearview mirror, her presence swelled inside him. The idea of Nicole not recognizing him and treating him like an average person absorbed him. He wanted to explore possibilities of a relationship with her. He might actually have pulled off seeing how a relationship "outside of his fame" worked, if he had fostered his deception over the course of a few months. But inside Grant's tornado of compressed time, he knew he felt safe with this girl; he liked her. He wanted a relationship—for him, the decision was made. Excitement fueled his anticipation of their subsequent meeting. He returned the next day to the lake and Nicole to confess his true identity and ask her to consider a liaison.

Picking up her hands, Grant looked straight into her heart. "I couldn't stop thinking about you last night. Hell, I couldn't remember all the words to our bleedin' songs, because I kept seeing you—yer face, yer hair, yer words—you." A curl of a smile tugged at his soft, smooth lips.

"Really? Me?" His words danced through Nicole's heart, hanging stars in her eyes.

But in erasing Gordon and revealing himself as Grant Henderson, the superstar poisoned his entire supposition. In rushing the process, Grant succeeded in doing the opposite of what he had wanted. He enticed her with the fairy tale—being carried off by a prince of the white-hot rock-and-roll kingdom! How could she want anything else? Then he sealed their agreement with a deep, reaching-down-to-her-toes kiss—her first ever.

He left Nicole standing in the dust from his rented red Sportster, holding on to his black leather Mary Quant driving cap. Grant Henderson pursued Nicole relentlessly over the next four weeks. Vases of shell-pink roses arrived weekly. An invasion of teddy bears filled her room. Nightly from the tour, he phoned her for hours.

Without a boy camping on their doorstep, Richard and Fran complacently winked at the attention, reducing it to a harmless, long-distance infatuation. They might have been able to battle the intrusion—after all, age was an issue: Grant was twenty-two and Nicole was sixteen—but in trying to protect Grant's notoriety, Nicole hid his actual identity from them.

Then tickets to Los Angeles for the Merseymen's closing concert of their US tour arrived. Alarmed that this had grown into more than a hormone-driven crush of some pimply-faced neighborhood kid, Richard demanded a full reckoning. Nicole confessed everything starting with their innocent meeting at the lake and concluded with an under-her-breath comment about the age difference.

The age disparity sent the Moores over the edge. They agreed to the trip only on the condition that Nicole first confess her age to Henderson. After all, what would an experienced twenty-two-year-old want with a teenager?

In her conversation with him that night, Nicole dressed up the fatal news in high heels and lipstick. "I'll be seventeen in four months. My birthday's in July."

Stunned silence robbed Grant of his voice. His hesitation stalled Nicole's heart. She fully expected to hear the click of his receiver.

Recovering Grant asked, "How much of a difference do our ages make to *you?*"

"It doesn't matter to me," a startled Nicole answered.

"I know it probably looks bad, but it doesn't change my feelings for you. If I have to wait… I will. But I need you now. Come to LA an' see for yerself what all the madness is about."

Romeo and Juliet may have thrown their dire differences to the wind, but the "age issue" greatly concerned Richard and Fran Moore and the Merseymen's manager, Bruce Eckstein. After talking, the adults on both sides cautiously agreed to an LA meeting.

Los Angeles loomed large before the family. Reluctantly, the Moores boarded the plane hoping their daughter would discover only a one-sided, schoolgirl fascination. However, Nicole went intent on solidifying a relationship, which she believed held the answers to her future. Riding in respectful silence, each side nurtured its own expectations. A nervous Eckstein waited for them in LA, hoping to quash the relationship before it leaked into the press and he had another mess to clean up, or before the Moores publicly filed charges for trifling with a minor.

However, the Moore family had no idea of the inexorable force waiting for them. The entire pop/rock scene played out in all its insane, glitzy glory before the unindoctrinated eyes of the threesome from rural Pennsylvania. Firsthand they experienced the throng of hundreds choking the entrance of the hotel. From the Merseymen's penthouse suite, they heard the delirium rise up from the street whenever one of *them* moved a curtain at the window. They suffered through the wall-to-wall screams at the concert, obliterating the group's music and singing. Because the Moores' had been sucked into the Merseymen's world, for their own safety they were subjected to the extreme cloak-and-dagger security needed to protect everyone.

From an adult point of view, Richard and Fran understood and acknowledged the negatives of celebrity. For teen Nicole, even though a hassle, she found the surreptitious shenanigans needed for protection engaging and intriguing. Sure she knew about the wrap parties following a concert, where the promoters used the lads to schmooze the local dignitaries with their chance to "see and be seen." She knew the LA tour closing bash would put Oscar Night to shame. And Nicole couldn't wait to experience it all from her special position on Grant's arm. But, that's when the promoter's opulent soiree personally slapped Nicole with fame's backhand.

In her parents' hotel suite just before leaving for the concert and its attending festivities, in the only few seconds of alone time they had, Grant struggled with a request. "'Bout this party gig later. The record bigwigs will be there, an' the band has to kiss up. I need you to kind of…ah…ah…be there, but…a…stand on your own. Get it?"

"Like we don't know each other?" Nicole questioned.

"Yes. No. I mean…sort of… Damn, can't you just wing it?" Grant wrestled with her inexperience to his routine. "'Member Ben, the bloke who works with sound that I introduced you to? He'll be there to take care of you." Grant tried to be patient.

Nicole nodded. "But will I ever get to see you?"

"Sure. I promise, babe." He flipped her his answer. "After the party…"

A roadie interrupted, dropping off a garment bag containing her "cover" for the evening.

"Cool. Yer get-up for the party. See ya, babe." Grant neatly slipped out.

Crushed by Grant's request and accompanying flippant attitude, Nicole collapsed on her bed. Tearfully, she totaled up the mounting disappointments Grant's notoriety forced her to swallow.

Her tears brought her father to her bedside. Not about to indulge her, he spoke with quiet authority. "Pretty tough welcome, huh? This is the adult world—Grant's world. He brought you here to see it. They don't do this just for a weekend, just for a lark. This is their 'butter and eggs,' and it's for keeps. In asking you to be his girlfriend, Grant wants you to make a decision—an adult decision. The decisions you make on this side of the fence will have far-reaching and permanent consequences. This is all coming sooner than we wanted or envisioned for you. There may be only five years' difference between your age and Grant's, but at this stage of your life, it's a world of separation. Just remember, you have a choice. You've been thrown into the deep end of the pool. You'll either sink, swim…or get out altogether. It's up to you."

Wallowing a moment more in self-pity, Nicole lay there pitting Grant's request against her father's words. When, from somewhere deep inside, she felt a stirring. Grit and determination welled up, forcing her to her feet. *Enough of this!* she scolded herself. *Tears aren't going to change things, and they certainly aren't going to help me make a decision. If Grant Henderson wants an adult, then he'll get an adult.* With confident defiance, Nicole marched into the bathroom to prepare.

Nicole recognized the "look" packaged inside the bag as that of the London model set. Better-heeled Brits derided them as "dollies," one step up from hookers. Her getup included a long straight pale-blond wig; a black leather miniskirt; a neon-yellow blousy shirt with matching tights; knee-high, high-heeled leather boots; gaudy chunky jewelry; and huge black plastic-rimmed saucer glasses. Nicole completed the disguise by donning Grant's leather driving cap.

The dolly bird persona also dictated a specific style of makeup. Washing her fresh face down the drain, Nicole applied the required milky foundation, then painted on the exaggerated upper and lower lashes, adding large amounts of shadow and coloring in her cheek line. Pale pink lipstick finished the package. She didn't recognize her image in the mirror, but that was the point. When the manufactured model emerged from the bath, Fran practically fell back in her chair. Weak-kneed, Richard sat down.

Sophisticated beyond her years, Nicole sauntered through the decadent party on Ben's arm. When a waiter pressed a champagne glass into Nicole's hand, Ben neatly replaced it with a glass of Pepsi. Ben pointed out the notables of the business. Each category of attendee had donned their appropriate uniform for the event. The all-powerful Label executives and producers wore Brooks Brothers. The movie stars, starlets, wannabes, and has-beens sparkled in their evening attire, while the moths of the press milled at the door. An array of groupies and hangers-on came in various states of undress. Nicole assumed them to be the hired escorts. They draped themselves over any unaccompanied celebrity, either for the moment or for the evening.

Once outside the glare of the spotlights or the view of the Label's suits, like a coach, Ben sent Nicole into the action at Grant's side. Then Grant got to pick up Nicole's hand or squeeze her close. Nicole watched carefully and learned.

Finally at three in the morning, drained of the exuberance of the day, Nicole and Grant came together, alone for the first time since their encounter at the lake. Huddled in the vacant stairwell just below the Merseymen's penthouse suite, they found enough solitude for conversation. Ben stood guard. For two hours, they discussed everything Nicole had witnessed over the past eighteen hours.

"What yer saw today is our world in the extreme, all the way 'round. The concert of a hundred thousand people and the fancy producer shindig aren't typical. But some version of it plays out in every city, after every gig. Yer know it. Yer read 'bout it in the rags. Yer hear it on the phone." Exhaustion permitted Grant honesty.

But Nicole's fear of challenging reality, and possibly losing her prince, kept her from asking about the girls and the groupies. Instead, she substituted, "What happens to me if I come along?"

"Our life—this life—becomes yours." Tenderly, Grant kissed her hand. "We'll still have to keep you a secret, but I'll be there for ya. We'll be together for each other, even if it is long distance. So how about it, then? Do you have my answer for me, luv?"

Nicole picked up the gauntlet Grant threw down, changing forever whatever destiny might have been hers. "You can count on me."

From Los Angeles, the Merseymen returned to London to start work on their first film as Nicole returned to her junior year at Oley Valley High School. But the solidification of their relationship only intensified Grant's focus. In June, timed to coincide with the end of her school year, first-class tickets to London arrived for Nicole and her parents. Fame had skewed Grant's outlook of life. At twenty-two, Grant Henderson had become accustomed to getting whatever he wanted. The two-week trip set up his actual objective; he wanted Nicole on the road with them for their summer tour.

Loud and long protests from her parents and Bruce Eckstein followed his proposal. Grant, however, anticipated all of them. Fran would accompany Nicole. They would travel apart from the Merseymen and become their "Managers of Internal Tour Relations." As such, Fran and Nicole would scout out in advance the various tour venues and bring the outside world back to the group. Then employing disguises, they would either smuggle the Boys out or the outside factions in. Since summer was Richard's busy traveling season anyway, he sacrificed his time with his wife for his daughter's extensive geography lesson.

By rearranging some meetings, Richard intercepted the tour in Amsterdam on July 19, 1964, Nicole's seventeenth birthday. Turning the family reunion to his advantage, Grant used the occasion to ask Nicole to marry him. Quickly, he followed his proposal with the promise they wouldn't marry until the following fall, well after Nicole had reached eighteen. Rather than a diamond, Grant slipped a ruby ring onto Nicole's right hand, because their engagement had to be a secret.

At the end of summer though, returning to the horse-and-buggy-paced life of the Oley Valley didn't hold the same excitement for Nicole it once did. High school sock hops and senior sleepovers couldn't compare to riding a comet across Europe. Listening to her friends prattle and coo over the latest teen mag's accounts of the Merseymen drove Nicole insane. She hated those magazines with their pages crammed full of awful pictures—pictures of beautiful, lean-bodied models hanging all over Grant. Oh, how those hurt!

Refusing to corral her spirit with moping, Nicole's lightning-in-a-jar enthusiasm propelled her. She kept busy, kept moving, with football games, school choir, and endless homework.

Halfway around the world, things weren't going as well for the Merseymen. Without Nicole's diversions, the tour had begun to grind. The group's press conferences lacked their spontaneous sparkle and notoriously biting wit. Already the cancer of low morale generated havoc for the tour.

In desperation, their manager phoned Richard and Fran. Frankly, the Moores couldn't have cared less. After the summer, they figured they had contributed quite enough to the *esprit de corps* of Henderson and his group. They weren't about to sacrifice Nicole's final year in school just to solve Eckstein's morale problem. While the Moores would rather not have indulged the relationship, they knew stopping it would have been as futile as halting a speeding freight train.

Bruce played his trump card by raising the specter of elopement. As he quickly reminded them, if pushed too far, it would be only a question of time before Grant seized upon that tempting solution. Both sides conceded it would be far better to control the situation rather than leave it to Grant's inevitable resourcefulness. Bruce had called to offer Nicole a permanent position as the Merseymen's Manager of Internal Tour Relations, complete with a salary.

The Moores countered with their own rigid demands: that Nicole complete her education and that she have a chaperone to ensure Grant didn't get carried away or worse yet, their daughter wouldn't become sexual fodder for the cadre who inhabited the music industry. The Moore's also negotiated a higher salary for Nicole to be paid weekly and an open-ended plane ticket back to Pennsylvania so she could return home anytime she felt the need, no matter what. Bruce concurred. The arrangement between the two factions infamously became known as *The Agreement*.

Accommodating the Moores' concerns, Bruce agreed to pay for a tutor/chaperone. Although the Moores were free to hire anyone, Eckstein highly recommended Ben's sister, Mary McDonough. She had grown up in the same area, knew the group, and conveniently lived in Virginia at William & Mary, where she taught English as a graduate assistant.

To cover all bases in case Nicole accepted the position, Richard and Fran scheduled a day for chaperone interviews. The following Wednesday, a woman in her midtwenties, of medium build, with shoulder-length chestnut hair caught at the neck in a band, wearing comfortable shoes, arrived. Richard took time off work to interview her. Curiosity snapping in Nicole's bright eyes drew her to her father's study door long enough for her to check out the stranger in the house before grabbing a kiss from her mom and dad, then popping out to catch her bus to school.

Over the course of the day, Richard and Fran interviewed several other candidates but called Mary back to offer her the position. Bruce's allotted salary nearly knocked Mary out of her chair. To that, the Moores themselves added an additional thousand dollars a month, an outstanding sum, to personally ensure Mary's adherence to their morality code and guarantee her loyalty to *their* daughter.

A gust of energy swept Nicole home from school slightly after three. Her innate commanding presence preceded her into the house. A flash, she dashed into the kitchen calling for her parents, happily dispensing news of her day as she hunted an audience to listen to her.

A tense "In here" from Richard summoned her to the study, where her parents' anxieties over the impending discussion deadened the air.

Reading the ominous room, Nicole instantly stilled her natural sparkle. Her clear alabaster skin paled. "What's going on, Daddy? Mommy?" she asked with trepidation. Dread kept her from asking about the woman stranger in the room.

"Have a seat, Nicole. We need to talk." Richard waved her into a chair.

Nicole slid her tall, willowy frame into one of the leather wing-back chairs. Gripping the chair arms, she strapped herself in for a bumpy ride. "Did someone die?"

"No. We need to discuss some things with you. It's about your future, Nicole," her mother answered. "We're concerned because at your age, decisions you make now can affect your whole life. Today, we're going to present you with one of those decisions."

Nicole's clench tightened on the chair, turning her knuckles an anxious white.

"Bruce called us several nights ago," her father began tautly. "He's offered you a position with the group performing the same type of duties you handled over the summer. If you accept, you'll have to give up your last year here in school. A tutor will be arranged for you. You'd tour with the Merseymen and would come home when they have holiday."

A wave of relief washed over her. *Is that the bad news? Bruce wants me back on tour?* Only her parents' sober faces tamped down her euphoria. For their sake, she dutifully maintained a thoughtful, rational façade.

Her mom pushed her slant on the topic. "You've already done the road thing. This will be your last year in school with your friends. Then everyone scatters on their different paths of life. If you go, you'll miss the football games, the dances and inevitably the lead in the school musical, *everything*. Those experiences will be gone forever. They will never come again. We don't want your answer right away. You need to consider *all* the consequences."

Her father interrupted, "We want you to spend some serious time weighing out this matter. Your decision will be forever. Think about it carefully. Take as long as you need." With that, they dismissed Nicole.

On her way out, she turned back to them. "What does Grant say?"

"He doesn't know anything about it, so there's no pressure. This is your decision and yours alone," her father replied.

In Nicole's absence, Mary and the Moores forced polite conversation as Nicole's parents struggled with the inevitable. Richard wasn't sure how long Nicole's decision would take. He was about to excuse Mary when Nicole reappeared in the doorway.

While her face reflected sobriety, her eyes betrayed unbridled joy. "I want to take the job."

Her dad challenged her. "And the logic behind your decision was...?"

"I'll only get one chance for a break like this. I want to take it."

"Did Grant or what he'd think influence your decision?" Fran asked.

"Well, I tried not to think about him," she answered truthfully. "It'll be great to be with him every day. But that will happen anyway when we get married next fall. You know I've always wanted to sing and perform. But I don't want to use my relationship with Grant to achieve that goal. With this job, if I work hard behind the scenes, maybe I'll get my chance. At least my foot will be in the door."

Dabbing her eyes with a tissue, Fran gestured toward Mary. "Then, Nicole, meet Mary McDonough. She'll be your tutor and your chaperone."

Before the two could really make a connection, Richard got down to business. "Nicole, you need to notify Bruce of your decision. He'll discuss a salary with you. Your mother and I feel a salary is important. It'll keep your position on a business level and afford you independence should the personal relationship sour. Under these circumstances, we don't want you to have to depend on Grant for money. The job also includes an open-ended plane ticket so you can come home *anytime* you need to leave. It's your escape hatch should you need to use it. No questions asked. Remember, whatever happens, we are always here for you." They may have regretted the timing of this decision for Nicole, but they knew they had raised a strong, independent young woman. Picking up Fran's hand, Richard escorted his wife from the study.

A variety of emotions paraded across Nicole's face as she talked with Bruce—surprise, thoughtfulness, giddy glee. The $1,200-a-week salary wowed her. Her part-time job at the local ice cream shop only netted her thirty a week. Finally coming up for air, one of Bruce's questions stopped her. Surprised, she turned the phone over to Mary. "Bruce wants to talk to you! Do you know him?"

Affirming their relationship with a smile, Mary then addressed Bruce on the phone. "Yes, Bruce, we've met. I suppose we'll go to the school tomorrow. Saturday? In Detroit? Yes, we can be there. Sure. Ta-ta for now." And she rang off.

Since the pair had only five days to prepare for months on the road, by tacit mutual assent, they put off further pleasantries until they accomplished the mountain of arrangements needed to meet the tour's schedule. From behind her winning smile, several times Mary caught Nicole summing her up. Would Mary be an iron-fisted warden or her ally?

The following morning after reviewing the tutor's credentials, the vice principal withdrew Nicole from her classes. They equipped Mary with Nicole's course specifications, textbooks, and reporting guidelines. By noon, Nicole Moore exited the doors of Oley Valley High School for the last time.

Mary and Nicole spent the few remaining days packing. Returning to Virginia, Mary organized everything according to seasons, packing in terms of trunks, not suitcases, then shipped them on ahead to their destination in Detroit. Meanwhile, Nicole did the same. On Saturday morning, they met up in the Moores' driveway as a cool fall wind blew into town.

Wearing cheery faces, Fran and Richard bravely dispatched their daughter, without lingering over their adieus. Just a brief hug and an "I love you," before the van ferried Nicole and Mary up and out the lane. Momentary apprehension over her monumental decision tugged at Nicole's heart as *Creekside* disappeared in the distance.

Once comfortably seated on the plane in first class, Nicole leaned over with her Pepsi for a toast. "Here's to a successful and enduring relationship, Mary." Hope radiated in her clear eyes. "Now maybe we can get acquainted."

Eagerness to make a connection arced inside Nicole. Rather than chew up time with trivia, Nicole reversed Mary's earlier notion of the teen's self-absorption by genuinely engaging her. "So who are you, Mary McDonough? And how does being stuck with me fit into your scheme of life?"

This glimpse of maturity both astonished and captivated Mary. She assured Nicole "stuck" wasn't the correct terminology. After answering thoroughly, Mary returned the focus to Nicole. She really wanted to get to know her charge.

Nicole energetically romped through her early memories of her parents, home life, and school, stopping to highlight her accomplishments and ambitions in music. The energy in her smile reflected her jubilant embrace of life. Her relationship with Grant lit her up. In a serious moment though, she confided her reasons for joining the group. "I really tried to let the gravity of the decision control me. But no matter how hard I enhanced the arguments for staying, the scale tipped overwhelmingly towards going and being an adult. Oh, Mary, this will be a real job—maybe even a stepping-stone to a singing career. This could open the door to something *big*. And such an opportunity will surely disappear if I turn it down."

Unexpectedly, Nicole, in a sober blink of her eyes, stopped abruptly. "Of course I realize that traveling with Grant will cement my chances of actually becoming Mrs. Grant Henderson. It will be harder for any of those flaming groupies or models to get their claws into my fiancé when I'm there to protect my territory. If I don't go, Mary, you know, I might lose him."

Whether she meant to or not, despite her exuberant exterior, in that fleeting instant, Nicole exposed her vulnerable side to Mary. In addition to a chaperone, Nicole needed someone to see her through all the confusing firsts in a maturing girl's life. It was then, beyond Bruce's handsome salary, the Moores' allotment, or *The Agreement*, Mary signed on in her heart to be Nicole's loyal confidant.

CHAPTER 3

★

The Road Ahead

When Mary and Nicole touched down in Detroit in the early afternoon, Ben met them at the airport.

Nicole leaped off the airstairs into his arms. "Ben! How great to see you. Did you hear the news? I'm here for good. C'mon, there's someone I want you to meet."

Oblivious to their sibling relationship, Nicole led him over to Mary. "I want you to meet my ol' bud, Ben. He kept me company at that big promoter party in LA and gave me the 'lowdown' on everybody there. Then he helped Mom and me pull off some great escapades over the summer."

"Hey, sis." Ben enfolded Mary in a brotherly hug. "Congrats on the job," he said as he jerked a familiar nod in Nicole's direction.

Amazement dropped Nicole's jaw. "You're—"

"Brother and sister. Sorry, we never got 'round to it. Do you mind terribly?" Mary inserted.

Nicole welcomed the relationship. "Cool! My new roommate is my pal's sister."

The three of them set to scheming how to pull off Nicole's surprise arrival. A first-class instigator in her own right, Nicole dreamed up an outrageous plan. To carry out the scheme, Ben secured a pair of roadie coveralls and hat for her. Once dressed, Nic tucked her hair up inside the hat. During the Merseymen's afternoon sound check in front of Bruce and a full crew, she bumbled her way onto the stage.

Keeping her face hidden by pulling the cap down low, she fixed her eyes on the floor.

Wham! She backed into Richie's drums.

Bang! She struck the strings on Pete's guitar.

Crash! A few guitar stands went flying.

Still focused on practice, the Merseymen muttered their complaints. But the more Nicole bungled, the louder and ruder their complaints grew.

Their increased complaining only worsened her fumbling. Finally, she got physical with them. Ricocheting off Jack, she careened into Pete. Backing up, she slammed into Grant.

Grabbing the errant roadie, Grant spun him around, giving him a good shake. "You bleeding loon, stop that! Get the hell off the stage!"

His forceful wrenching shook off Nicole's cap, releasing her hair. Swinging her head around, coming up face-to-face with Grant, Nicole beamed at him. "Surprise!"

From their seats in the audience, Bruce and his assistants rocked with laughter. The realization finally dawned on Grant and his bandmates.

Grinning, Grant grabbed up Nicole in his arms. The others rushed over to congratulate her on the good joke. Never ones to miss a chance to party, Nicole's arrival demanded a celebration.

Settling back into their dressing rooms, Pete pried, "So you missed us, eh?"

"Come for a bit of a visit, did ya?" from Jack.

"Actually I'm here for good," Nicole bubbled.

Incredulous, Grant asked, "What do you mean 'for good'?"

Bruce stepped in with the explanation. "You blokes were so down in the mouth, I figured we could all use a good giggle. We had a great go this summer, so I brought her back."

Momentarily holding her breath, Nicole hoped they approved of her intrusion.

In a boisterous hoot, the group made themselves a party. Pete called front for food. Jack played bartender. Cheerfully pulling Nic onto his lap, Richie hauled out a pair of sticks and set the beat on the coffee table to Nicole's scat singing. Picking up his guitar, Grant coaxed out the melody. Pete plinked harmonizing chords on the piano, while Jack noodled around on his harmonica. The world erupted into a spur-of-the-moment Merseymen-plus-one concert! What incredible chemistry between these seasoned rock stars and this fresh-from-the-farm girl of Pennsylvania!

The inevitability of the evening concert broke the party apart. Grant slid his arm about Nicole's waist. Pulling her tight to him, he leered. "Cor! I can't believe yer here. Bet on it, we've more celebratin' to do later."

Not wishing to dampen spirits, Bruce suggested Nicole stay for the concert, rather than hiding out in the hotel room as she had done over the summer during the show. "No reason you shouldn't nip into the blond wig again and participate in the festivities this evening. The gear is waiting for you in the next room." Smugly the manager chortled, clearly heartened by the abrupt change in the attitudes of his lads.

Briefly slipping out of the room, Nicole returned wearing the long straight pale-blond wig and one of the "dolly" getups from the summer. Kicking out her long-booted leg, the alter ego of Nicole Moore performed a modeling spin. "What do you think? Pretty fab, huh?"

"Oh, that is positively awful, isn't it?" Grant groaned. "But unfortunately necessary if you want to be with us in public at the concert." Once again, he lustily grabbed her up, his brown eyes flashing. "Oh, I can't wait to get you out of that crap!"

Grant's comment clanged in the chaperone's ears. In the early days, before leaving Liverpool for school, Mary had also hung around the cellar clubs with Ben. Familiar with these cheeky lads from Mersey Town, she recognized some of their risqué chatter as an affect—some wasn't. Not sure how to take it, Grant's remarks chaffed her.

As concert time neared, Nicole noted the familiar routine endured: preshow interviews, pictures and autographs, the concert, postshow audiences, and finally the promoters' wrap party. As always, excessive knots of groupies clogged up everything.

But afterward in the Hotel Pontchartrain, Bruce reserved the entire top-floor restaurant, complete with a lavish buffet, unlimited supply of bubbly, and the hotel's band for their private party. An assistant let in the few lucky beauties culled from the day's pack to act as "escorts." Popping the first cork on the champagne, Jack proposed a toast. Lifting their glasses, they toasted the new team and the road ahead, as the welcome-back party shifted into high gear.

In her first time out as a chaperone, Mary managed her position from a distance. From her conversations with Bruce and Ben, she kept Nicole in sight throughout the whirl of the evening.

Once away from the prying eyes of the press, Grant very quickly stripped Nic of the blond wig. Running his fingers through her dark tresses, he teased them back to life. Grant also ignored all intrusion from any outsiders. Incredibly enough, the other girls seemed deflected from sidling up to wheedle autographs or conversation. Even Pete, Jack, and Richie, who practiced the one-for-all philosophy, kept their distance.

Grant proficiently executed the duties of escort. Realizing champagne was a new experience for her, he encouraged Nic to nurse glasses of water along with sips of bubbly. He paced her alcohol consumption by sensually feeding her tastes of food—interspersing the hors d'oeuvres with kisses. Watchdog Mary suspicioned his motives. It raised her hackles as he slow-danced with Nicole with his hands clasped at the small of her back, their hips locked together while he nuzzled her neck with kisses.

Around three, all the rest paired off and began to disappear. Only Jack and two members of the hotel's band remained, heads together, drinking and dueling away.

With an iced bottle of champagne and Nicole in tow, Grant headed toward Mary. "Mary dear, Nic is beginning to look a little under the weather—first time with champagne and all. So she won't suffer in the morning, would you be a dear and find her some bicarbonate?"

Nicole's swimming eyes told Mary that Grant was right. "Why don't *you* get the bicarb? *I'll* take Nicole back to her room," Mary countered.

"And where do you expect me to come up with the seltzer? You know I can't go mucking about the hotel," Grant whined. "No, *I'll* take her to the room. *You* get the seltzer."

Heading off in different directions, Mary felt uneasy about separating herself from them, but of course she realized Grant's celebrity precluded him from wandering about the hotel.

However, Mary's absence freed Grant to implement his personal agenda. While the elevator endlessly clicked off the floors, Nicole and Grant shared sweet, sloppy kisses. Arriving at the room, Nic's heart thumped feverishly as Grant slipped the key from his pocket to open the door.

Confused, she looked at him. "Grant, this isn't my room."

"I know, luv." He kissed her once, then again. "I can't be seen down on your level. So I got the key to Jack's room. He's busy now and won't need it. You can rest here until Mary gets back with the seltzer."

With her head buzzing, Nicole swallowed his story.

Shutting the door behind them, the tiny bathroom nightlight faintly illuminated the hotel room's entryway, creating light-edged shadows. Grant fumbled to put down the champagne, then drew Nic tightly to him. His building passion of the evening exploded. He deluged her with kisses. For Nicole, the evening's champagne had weakened her moral resolve and spawned an unfamiliar appetite. Hungry for him, she returned every one of his kisses. Their breaths came in feverish pants as they tried to devour each other. All new to her, she continued to cover him with kisses. Drawing away slightly, he held her in his eyes, ablaze with desire. Innocent with trust, Nicole stared back at him. His hands moved to the top button of her blouse. One button slipped through the hole and opened. She let out a slight gasp; he tenderly kissed it off her lips—their eyes riveted on each other. His fingers, with sight of their own, deliberately moved down to the next button in line and released it. Silently, he checked her resolve with another kiss, then proceeded. The next button fell to his fingers, and the next, the next, and the final one. With her blouse gaping open, in one seamless movement, he pulled off his turtleneck, baring his chest. Grant returned to her mouth, kissing her tenderly, still testing her intention, then pressed in closer. His kisses grew longer and deeper, increasing in intensity and fervor. A tinge of alarm crept inside of Nicole. Sensing her change, Grant lightened up and returned to sweet, lingering kisses to ease her edginess. Nic gasped, stepped back, and landed, thud up against the door. His determination steeled. Gathering her up in his arms, Grant suffocated her with kisses, trying to stifle any thoughts of rejection.

A distant noise broke through the fog of passion.

"Nicole. Nicole. Are you in there?" Mary's panicked knock pleaded. Realizing she had been hoodwinked, frantically, the chaperone had knocked on door after door along the corridor of the Boys' suites, until sounds of little bumps and thuds brought her to Jack's door.

Shushed silence greeted her raps.

"What the bloody hell?" Grant demanded in a whisper.

"It's Mary!" Nicole blurted.

"How in the freakin' hell did she find…"

"Mary?" Nicole answered as frenzied scrambling by the pair ensued. "Just a minute."

Wondering how late she'd been, Mary scolded herself for letting Grant dupe her.

"We're coming!" Grant growled. "What the…"

Nicole opened the door as quickly as possible to ease Mary's suspicions.

Stepping past her innocent charge, Mary came up in Grant's face. Fire shot from her eyes, even as she kept her tone level. "Don't *ever* try a stunt like that again. In the future, you will respect me, my position, and Nicole—*Mister* Henderson. I expect you to live up to your portion of *The Agreement*. Do I make myself clear?"

Then she stepped into the hallway. "Come on, Nicole, let's find our room."

With his turtleneck back on and the champagne bottle in hand, Grant cursed bitterly as he slid by them. "I'll see you tomorrow!" he threatened. Heatedly, he foisted the key into Mary's hand. "Here, you lock up."

Embarrassed, crushed by being manipulated into the middle of an awkward situation she really didn't understand, Nicole sputtered a few apologetic explanations.

Mary knew how she handled the situation would set the timbre of their relationship. Rather than using lectures or disapproving looks, once in their room, she fixed Nicole the bicarbonate along with aspirin, then settled her down with a quiet discussion about the womanly stirrings inside her. Drawing from personal experience, Mary explained those feelings and what had happened, how Nicole got tangled up in a situation pitting Grant against her. From their conversation, she could tell Nicole desperately cared about her opinion and wanted Mary as her ally. Although they never mentioned the incident again, Mary knew Nicole understood her parameters.

Turning out the light, staring up at the ceiling, Mary berated herself for losing control of the situation.

Nicole broke the silence with a soft, quavering voice. "Mary, is it normal that every time I think about Grant I feel prickly hot and have trouble catching my breath?"

"Yes, that's normal."

"Do you think Grant feels the same way?"

"I don't know, Nic," she answered. But Mary did know.

Up at eight getting their things together, Mary let Nicole sleep until the phone jangled her awake at nine. The group had to be in Chicago by noon. Going up to "the suite" for breakfast, everyone there looked like hell. Recognition came through slits of barely opened, bloodshot eyes. Nicole couldn't tell if Grant resented her for last night or suffered from too much party like everyone else. Mary nursed Nic along with water, orange juice, and aspirin.

By the time Mary and Nic boarded the plane, everyone else seemed remarkably recovered and energetic. Thanks, no doubt, to the multicolored "vities" the rest popped at breakfast. "Vities" designed to help them endure extremely aberrant, exacting schedules, to put them to sleep at the appropriate times and wake them up shortly thereafter. Vities whose street names were "dexi" and "benny" along with a few others, whose effect couldn't be shaken even in normal times or on vacation. Grant, Mary, and the rest of the "Boys" stridently kept these "vities" from Nicole.

Tamely, Grant held the seat next to him open for Nicole. Sliding the armrest out of sight, he nestled her in the crook of his arm. "Go ahead and doze if you can," he comforted. Nicole had only an hour more to recuperate before Chicago appeared, and the fray began again, with no time for hangovers.

Coming to grips with the situation, Mary realized that Grant was basically still a hormone-driven kid whose sexual fantasies had been satisfied beyond most men's wildest dreams. With all those groupies hanging around, the band didn't exactly live like monks. She understood how it genuinely impressed Grant that Nicole didn't recognize him at first, and later she didn't hang on him because of his name. Grant, at that stage of his life, was very much a little boy lost. He found himself uprooted from home, cut off from people and family he could trust, adrift in a rapidly spinning whirlpool without a secure port. In the immediate, his drive for security surpassed his sexual appetite. He had latched on to Nicole because she captured his interest by being a rock, not a leech. Only after a few months on the tour did he grow comfortable enough to take the security she offered for granted. Then, she became a challenge. Short of attaching herself to Nicole at the wrist, Mary had to create ways to intrude without being a warden. She worked at building a bond of trust with Nicole. In the process, they became best friends.

When the guys left for the concert site, Mary and Nicole cracked the books, which usually afforded them about six hours of class time. Mary enhanced her tutoring by using Nic's forays into the different towns for the Merseymen as fact-gathering scavenger hunts. In addition to bringing the city back to the group, her assignments included researching the particulars about each locale's history.

Sure, Nicole studied, but she worked at her position with the Merseymen in one mode—flat out. Although she possessed an innate business sense, Nic pursued her own agenda. Desperately, she knew she wanted to sing, but trading on her insider connection to get it distressed her. She found it difficult to even mention it to Grant or anyone else in the group, lest they see her as using them just to advance her personal agenda. To gain her own toehold in the business, she constantly pestered Bruce over subtleties of the business, always wanting to grasp more.

In mid-October, the tour headed to Mexico City, Guadalajara, and Acapulco, continuing down into South America and into their springtime. Hopscotching across the continent, places like Rio with their nude beaches and hot Latin attitudes only increased carnal frustration between Grant and Nicole. Maturing, Nic learned the joke about cold showers.

The last week of November, the tour wrapped and flew to Miami. From there, the Merseymen would head back to Britain and into the recording studio until Christmas. Nic would rejoin them for the opening of their winter tour in Paris on New Year's Eve.

A miserable Grant approached Nicole on their last night together in Miami. Under the night's cloak, they walked the hotel's private beach with the waves quietly lapping against the sand. Peering out over the white foam into the inky blackness stretching to infinity, Grant moaned, "It's almost four weeks until I see you again. How can I live without you? I can't do this."

"You'll be just across these waves. It's like being just across my lake," Nic stated bravely.

"Yeh right! Do you know how far 'just across' is? It's four thousand bloody miles, five time zones, and an eternity away!"

Hoping to brighten his mood, Nicole asked Grant what he wanted for Christmas.

"You *know* what I want," he retorted, his eyes smoldering. Unconsciously, he fiddled with the ruby engagement ring on her hand, then looked up into her eyes. "Marry me!"

"I'm going to."

"No, not someday. Now! Over the holiday. Let's get married Christmas Eve."

"Oh, that's such a wonderful idea. Yes! Yes, let's do it." But a thought halted Nicole's fantasy. "What about my age, Bruce, and my parents? Can we do it?"

"I dunno. Let's go ask." Grabbing her hand, they sprinted for Bruce's room.

Grant paused before knocking. "You know, we don't *have* to ask."

"How's that?" Nicole didn't catch his meaning.

"Vegas! It's only six hours away." Grant returned bursting with his discovery.

"Elope? I can't." She couldn't believe he offered it. She saw her dream of a fairy-tale wedding vaporize before her eyes.

"Why not?"

"Grant, my parents! It would devastate them," Nic protested.

"Okay, so we'll ask." He rapped at Bruce's door.

Bruce met their request cautiously. "I had hoped that the careers of the group would be more entrenched before we throw another wife at the public. You know we started this ride with Jack being married… Well, I guess we're as solid as we can be. Now is as good a time as any… Okay, as long as Nicole's parents agree." Bruce offered his hand, then clasped Grant about the shoulders. Kissing Nicole's cheeks, he blessed in his best Yiddish, "*Mazel tov.*"

CHAPTER 4

★

The Fairy Tale

Home—*Creekside*. The trees stood bare against the slate November sky hung with threatening snow clouds. The house felt less familiar, like it didn't recognize her. A cool tingle of panic pinched Nicole's stomach. *What if my parents say no?*

Sensing her dread, Grant wrapped an arm around Nicole. He kissed her forehead to chase away the uneasiness. "Ready? We *can* do this."

Opening the door, Nic called as they stepped inside, "Mom, Dad, we're home."

Fran greeted them in the kitchen with kisses. Putting on the kettle for tea, she urged them to sit. The aroma of sweet familiarity perfumed the kitchen. Scents of cinnamon, vanilla, and ginger from Fran's Christmas baking spiced the air. She set a sample plate before them while making small talk.

Richard's steps came quickly on the stairs. "Is that Nicole's voice I hear? You're here already?"

"Hi, Daddy!" Nicole jumped up to give him a hug and a kiss, like in the past.

Rising to his feet, Grant extended his hand.

"Well…and Grant too." He addressed Grant with an air of surprise and caution. "I thought Nicole said you'd be heading back to England?"

"There's been a slight change in plans, Mr. Moore. I thought I'd see Nicole home and drop in for a bit of a chat."

Richard read between the lines. Seating himself at the kitchen table squarely across from Grant, he readied himself for this exchange between the men. "So what brings you here, Grant?"

Out of control of the situation, afraid it would spiral horribly wrong, Nicole attempted to jump in; but the pressure from her mother's hands pinching into her shoulders hushed her. Fran also knew the participants of this dance.

"I've come for your permission, sir, to change the date of our wedding." Perspiration accumulated along Grant's brow.

"Any particular reason you're asking?" Nic's dad fished, staring him down.

"Yes, sir." Grant reached for Nicole's hand. "I love Nicole, and I don't want to be apart from her anymore."

Skeptical, Richard wagged his head. "I don't understand the rush, Grant. She already travels with you. You're constantly together."

"Mr. Moore, I'm tired of not having her by my side. Tired of not being able to hold her close because someone might see. We travel separately. I can't go out with her unless one of us wears a disguise. I want to kiss her and not care if a man with a camera catches us. I want to cradle her in my arms as I fall asleep. I love her. I have since that day at the lake. And, sir… *The Agreement* is getting more difficult to live with." Grant lowered his voice to a man-to-man tone. "I think you know what I mean, sir."

Disturbed, Fran drew in an audible breath. "Grant, is that the only reason to move up the wedding? Please…the truth."

Grant's eyes sparked. "Yes, ma'am! You have my word. We've not been together."

"I believe you," Fran retreated. "I believe you."

Richard pressed his agenda. "If you get married now, what happens to Nicole's education?"

"That would continue. I wouldn't jeopardize her education. Mary will remain as her tutor."

"And college?"

"The same, sir. I'd make it my personal responsibility," Grant bartered.

Persisting, Richard leaned in. "What about her job and her salary? Or since you're getting married, would you dissolve that arrangement?" he accused.

Those questions stunned Grant. He never considered Nicole's employment. Bruce handled that side of the equation. "I... I see no reason for any of that to change. I will personally guarantee her position and salary," he complied.

"A raise would be nice too," Richard trumped.

Grant nodded his acquiescence.

The Christmas Eve date—a mere twenty-six days away—however, left her parents scrambling. Grant understood there would be unusual expenses attached to the wedding because of his celebrity status. He made it clear he expected to bear the entire financial obligation of the wedding. Giving Nicole carte blanche, happily he departed, leaving her in her driveway with a kiss and his parting words. "I'll be back on the twenty-third. I promise I won't think of anything else the entire time. Nicole, plan the wedding of your dreams. Money is no object. I'll send someone to help."

The logistics of planning a wedding to a major rock sensation in total secrecy proved daunting. A large city, such as Philadelphia, offers anonymity among its masses. But in a rural community of thirty-five hundred, trying to mask the small army needed for lodging, catering, and transportation embodied a ton of complexities. Grant's generous wallet greatly eased the process. They decided the best way to camouflage the affair was to hide it in the open. Richard suggested they explain the influx of visitors and foreigners as clients he had invited to an elaborate Christmas soiree. Because of security concerns, Nicole eliminated all her lifelong friends from the bridal party and the guest list. For added privacy, the Moores decided to host the reception at the house. Even a pared-down guest list contained fifty invitees.

Without ever selecting her colors or choosing the first flower, the logistics of celebrity ate up five precious days of their tight time frame. Finally, Nicole got down to shaping the wedding itself. She asked Mary to be her maid of honor; Jack's wife, Candy, would be an attendant; and Jack Junior would be the ring bearer. Grant chose his brother Robert as his best man and Jack to escort Candy and represent the group.

In the afternoon of December 6, Vada Knight and her assistant descended from London. Vada epitomized the personification of an eccentric designer with wild flaming-red hair and flowing layers of splashy-colored clothes. Numerous haute couture houses on the Continent and glitterati from all over the globe clamored for her genius. Grant had tapped her not only to design the wedding clothes, but to help fashion the entire celebration. Sweeping into the living room, sketch pad in hand, Vada trailed fabric swatches and ideas of designs with which to create the perfect fairy-tale wedding.

Dismissing the obvious Christmas colors, Vada selected a color palette of deep blue with white and silver garnish. Transferring her wedding fantasy to paper, Vada rubbed her hands together. "Ah, you'll be the perfect princess." She created a streamlined version of the Dickens era, crafting the dresses out of moire taffeta, Nicole's in ivory, the attendants in the rich winter blue.

Vada preached the credo of sensual experiences, believing that a memorable experience touched as many of the senses as possible. "Flowers," she exclaimed with her arms thrown open, grandly encompassing a wide swath as she walked. "We will have lots and lots of flowers—extravagant quantities! Ahh, their wondrous perfume, their lavish colors—especially in the dead of winter!"

Vada stayed only for two days; but in her wake, she left reams of instructions for the floral arrangements, the church, the music, and the reception.

Grant phoned daily. His calls brought news of the Merseymen's business. Ripe with ideas, they had breezed through their recording sessions. They had enough material for a new album with another under way. Bruce had approved a script and signed another movie deal—filming would begin at the end of the winter tour. Listening to Grant's magical recitation reduced Nicole's wedding plans to the mundane.

On their last night alone together as a family, and the first moment of peace without wedding demands intruding, a twinge of conscience poked Nicole as she finished washing the dinner dishes. Standing next to her mother at the sink, she fished for loose silverware in the dishwater. "Mom, what do you really think of my marrying Grant?"

Fran thoughtfully paused. "He's a wonderful lad, and he seems sincere. But I feel we hardly know him. I wish you could have met him about six years from now, after you finished college. That way your career would be started, and you would know what it was like to be on your own for a while. But…that never really was an option, was it? Not after Grant came along."

"Am I wrong?"

"That's not mine to say. I'm only saying that I would have preferred you wait until much later." Pausing again, this time she proceeded with great hesitancy. "No matter what happens"—she threw a glance heavenward—"God forgive me for saying this—there will be enough money to provide you with a future. You will always have a means of independence now. We could have given you college, but Grant has the wherewithal to give you not only college but also contacts to connect you to your future. You have always aspired to a singing career. God blessed you with that natural ability. But only you have the power to turn those assets to your benefit, and that will come through wise choices. Don't stray from your belief in God and always be faithful to His commands and yourself."

Her mom's mercenary candor rocked Nicole. "What about love? You didn't mention Grant loving me—only money!"

Her mom patted Nicole's soapy hand. "Love—its absence or presence—is something only you can answer. Only you know how you feel about each other. Search your heart. You know the answer."

"Is this just girl talk, or can an old man get in on this conversation too?" Richard asked, entering the kitchen.

Fran turned from the sink. "Nicole wanted my thoughts on her marrying Grant."

"Having second thoughts?" her father asked. "Of course, every father thinks his baby is too young, but I trust your decision. I hope everything turns out as you think it should. Marriage is never easy. And you are not saddling yourself with an average situation. Grant and his lifestyle bring a lot of extra baggage. This is not a cozy-house-with-a-white-picket-fence relationship you are going into, is it now?"

Questions crinkled Nicole's nose. She didn't understand.

Her dad continued. "I mean, you won't have just the typical 'learning to live with someone' pressures of marriage. You will have all those, plus traveling around the world, plus life at the speed of light, compounded by the universe and the press watching, waiting—and hoping you'll fall. It's a lot to cope with, but you've always been resilient and resourceful. You have great inner strength, and when you need it, you'll find it... Why all the questions now anyway? Are you getting cold feet? Because up until you say 'I do,' it's never too late to call this thing off. We won't think less of you if you do."

Nicole snuggled into Dad's open arms for a hug. "No, it's just that we never really had a chance to talk. I wanted to make sure how the two of you felt."

"We love you, that's how we feel," Fran and Richard echoed, as they all retreated to the family room and watched the yard fill up with snow.

The final avalanche of details crashed in on them in the morning when Vada Knight, two of her associates, and twelve massive trunks arrived. Greeting them with exuberant hugs and air kisses, Vada excitedly teased, "Oh, Princess, do I have surprises for *you*!"

After setting up operations in the Moores' basement, Vada enlisted Fran to direct the small battalion amassed to assemble and decorate the reception tent. The huge white canvas tent engulfed most of the manicured portion of the backyard. Tall branches, tiny white lights, and flecks of silvery glitter created a winter forest fantasy inside the tent. Centerpieces lavished with white roses, blue delphinium, and waxy-green holly spread their magic across the navy linen tablecloths and around the bone china and cut crystal.

Then Vada focused her attention on their country church. The muddle of musicians, florists, decorators, and a stage manager over-ran the quaint stone chapel. Vada flitted here and there, her gown in a whirl to catch up, directing one operation, then interrupting herself to take up the reins on another.

Numb from the excess of morning activities, Nicole sat in the church watching the production unfold.

"Do you actually like hanging out in churches?" a warm whisper came from behind her.

Nicole turned to discover Grant's soft brown eyes. Forgetting her surroundings, she jumped up and threw her arms around him. "Did you come to rescue me?"

"No, luv, I came to join you. I hear we have a wedding here tomorrow."

"You're early. Are the rest of the guys and Bruce with you?"

"Yeah. The drivers took them to the house."

"Candy and Mary get in all right?"

He nodded. "They are at yer mum's house."

"What about your parents and family? I can't wait to meet them..."

"Relax, luv. Everyone is here, and we are all organized. You've hired a marvelous crew of meddlers."

On his way up the aisle to toe Vada's mark, the minister stopped long enough to address the couple. "Ah, the impetuous Romeo has joined us I see," he commented as he slipped by.

Turning his attention back to Nicole, Grant asked, "Do you need to be here? Let's face the music and get the marriage license business out of the way."

This was the only breach in their logistics of secrecy. No subterfuge could be employed here; they had to use their legal names in filing for the license. If Grant were recognized, all their careful planning would be up in smoke, and their wedding day would be lost in a world-gone-mad media frenzy. In an effort to escape detection, Grant put on his leather driving cap, letting it ride up high on his forehead, with his bangs tucked up inside. Avoiding direct eye contact, they completed the forms, fearing that any moment they'd be met with the delirium that follows identification. Keeping his answers brief, Grant responded to the clerk's questions with a simple yes or no to conceal his accent.

Operating in robotic bureaucratic rote, the older clerk never looked up or attempted polite conversation. In the end, she formalized the document with a cold silver seal.

Despite the mounting pressures of last-minute details and the rehearsal, Grant requested a final ride to the lake. "It all began there. I really want to go back once more before the dream becomes reality."

Nicole couldn't refuse him. Saddling Thunder and her dad's horse, the pair rode out to the lake. A thin veil of ice covered most of the water's surface. Grant brushed off a log where they sat amid their remembrances of that fateful day in March.

"I wanted to give you my Christmas present before the hubbub of tomorrow swallows up the day." Grant brought forth a small box wrapped in Christmas green.

"I don't believe how our minds work together." Nicole pulled out a small package of her own and handed it to him. "Open yours first."

His fingers deftly opened the box, revealing a gold medallion and chain. Inscribed on the face, "I *agree* to love you forever. Nicole." Tears stood in his eyes, and he embraced her. "You've changed *The Agreement*. Oh, I definitely approve. How I love you!

"Now it's your turn."

Carefully untying the bow, Nicole lifted the lid of the box. The sun flashed back into her eyes. A heart-shaped two-carat diamond solitaire blazed in the sunlight.

"I always wanted you to have a proper diamond instead of that lame birthstone ring for our engagement. Now we don't have to be afraid of anyone seeing." Taking the ring from its bed, Grant got down on one knee. "This time with a real diamond—will you marry me?"

Nicole recovered her breath enough to whisper, "Yes." Admiring the ring on her left hand ring finger, she fell into his waiting arms and met his lips.

Running slightly behind schedule, and with her bride and groom AWOL, Vada stood vigil in the driveway, arms crossed, the multiple layers of her dress fluttering in the breeze. Her glare tracked the approaching couple all the way down the drive. "Where have you been? Who gave you permission to ride off into the sunset? We have a wedding to rehearse—or weren't *we* going to participate?"

Smiling, Grant dismounted as he went to appease the angry goddess.

During the rehearsal party, Grant questioned Nicole about her side of the guest list. Dutifully, she reported only her closest relatives would be in attendance because of the privacy considerations.

"But yer mates—er, yer friends. Did you invite any of them?"

"Of course not—security, you know."

"Then do it, luv. Do it. The three friends you were so close to, wouldn't it be gear if they could be there?" Grant prodded.

Nic nodded hesitantly. "But the security…"

"Damn the security, Nicole. Do it! Call them now. Invite them!" Leading her to a phone, he picked up the receiver and handed it to her. "Call!" Grant urged. "And remember it's Christmas Eve. They should bring their families."

Of Leanne, Annie, and Cookie, she dialed Cookie's number first, all the time considering how she would explain the situation yet keep the secret.

Nicole's wedding day dawned with a hint of snow in the air. Slipping on her robe and climbing inside a pair of warm slippers, she proceeded to the kitchen where her mom and dad greeted her along with the aroma of fresh cinnamon rolls. She expected the household to be a hotbed of activity, but serenity reigned. As her mom poured tea, she informed Nicole of the itinerary. "The hairdresser will be here at eleven. Vada and her associates will meet us at the church at two thirty to dress."

Folding the newspaper, Richard laid it down alongside his plate and handed his cup to Fran for a refill. "So how's the bride this morning?"

Nicole mimicked a shiver. "A little nervous, but fine."

Her dad pushed a tiny box in her direction. "It's not a Christmas present, just something we wanted you to have." Her mother joined them at the table.

Nicole opened the box to reveal an elegant lavaliere, in a gold turn-of-the-century setting. A pearl sat in the middle of the solid-gold heart, surrounded by delicate gold filigree. "Oh, it's so beautiful. Thank you. Can I wear it today?" She kissed each of them.

"We hoped you would. I know it's not silver to match everything else, but it belonged to your grandmother Moore. It was a wedding present from your grandfather to her. She gave it to me when I married your father, and now it's your turn," her mom responded.

Several times that morning, Fran turned the nervous Nicole away from the doors overlooking the backyard preparations. By the time Nicole bent over the sink for the hairdresser to shampoo her hair, her stomach had parked itself in her throat. With her head under running water, she never heard the doorbell ring. The next thing she knew, Cookie tapped her on her arm.

"Okay, Nicole, I can't stand it any longer," she huffed. "I didn't sleep a wink all night. So tell me who are you marrying?"

Begging indulgence from the hairdresser, Nic substituted her mom getting shampooed so she could temporarily turn her attention to Cookie.

Once out of earshot, Cookie burst, "It's Gordon. I'm right, aren't I?"

"No, Cookie. Come with me, and I'll explain the entire thing." Up in Nic's room, she sat Cookie down. "I'm marrying Grant Henderson."

"Who's he? He's not from around here, is he? Did you meet him over the summer?" The reality sat so far outside the realm of possibility that recognition totally escaped her.

"Grant Henderson, of the Merseymen," Nic prompted.

Cookie's eyes grew huge in surprise. She made the connection. "No! You're kidding! Not *the* Grant Henderson!"

Briefly, Nic stepped Cookie through the entire story. She noticed the more she talked about the upcoming event and shrieked along with Cookie, her nervousness abated.

Finally, Nic could hear the hairdresser calling for her presence again.

"Oooh, I can't believe this," Cookie confessed as she hugged Nic goodbye. "I'm thrilled for you. I'm so glad your mom called me to come over this morning. See you this afternoon. Ooh, Grant Henderson—wow!" Then out she slipped.

A light snow began to fall as they arrived at the church. Lush garlands of white flowers outlined the entry arch and wrapped all the handrails—a hint of what waited inside. What a transformation! It stole Nicole's breath. White roses, deep-blue delphinium, and lush amounts of green holly leaves tumbled from every available space, saturating the chapel with their heavenly aroma. Vada had fulfilled her promise of surprise. From the decorations, to the specially designed pearl tiara for Nicole's three-yard veil, and even a horse-drawn sleigh to carry the couple off to the reception—Vada had far surpassed any fantasy Nicole could have dreamed. She created a new standard by which fairy tales would forever be judged.

But the day wasn't just about fluff and frills. Nicole's most enduring memory of that day remained Grant's expression while they exchanged their vows. How Grant's eyes sparkled with sincerity as the minister placed her hand in his. He emanated sober earnestness as he meaningfully repeated each phrase of their vows. Grant locked onto Nicole's heart when he said, "I do."

The reception heaped more icing onto the already incredible Christmas wedding fantasy. The servers paraded their bounty on hefty silver platters like servants of old at a king's feast. Crown roasts, flaming desserts, trays spilling fresh tropical fruit, and continually flowing champagne circled the guests to the winter garden. Sprinkled throughout the evening, the recurrent tinkle of crystal called for the bride and groom to kiss.

Grant delighted in introducing the Merseymen to awestruck Cookie, Leanne, and Annie. On numerous occasions, he hailed Ben and made sure the girls had every photo they wanted taken with the group.

Following the meal, Grant and the rest of the Merseymen approached the orchestra. Assuming their positions, Grant stepped to the mic. "Mr. Moore, could you please bring Nicole down front." Richard led Nicole to where the group stood, positioning her alongside Grant.

Grant began again, "I've been working on this material for a while. I wrote this song for my beautiful wife. I'd like to sing it in public for the first time tonight. Nicole, luv, this is for you." Grant slipped the microphone from its stand and with the introductory chords began "On This Day I'm Yours Forever." Pouring out his heart, he sang his love song to his bride. Nicole could hardly see him through the pool of tears that filled her eyes. His devotion reduced her to putty. Following the performance, waiters passed out piano-shaped black lacquer music boxes that played the melody of Grant's ballad to each of the guests as a memento of the occasion.

Because it was Christmas, and because of the overwhelming British contingent, in addition to the wedding cake, the chef produced a wonderful plum pudding for dessert. The waiters wheeled the pudding to the center of the floor while the guests, arm in arm, encircled it and sang "Good King Wenceslas." Igniting the pudding, a chorus of "We Wish You a Merry Christmas" closed the evening.

A final surprise waited on Nicole's bed when she changed for their departure. Vada left a divine white velvet going-away dress. And inside Nic's suitcase was an elegant negligee of white silk, bordered with lace, trimmed in satin. Each creation bore the designer's label—Vada's farewell surprise.

Once Grant finished changing, he knocked at Nicole's bedroom door. "Ready, luv?" he questioned, opening her door.

"Do you realize," Nicole commented, looking around her childhood room, "this is the last time this will be my room?" With a touch of melancholy, she ran her fingers across some memories on her desk.

Fearing getting bogged down, Grant nodded. "I know. C'mon. They're waitin'."

With the toss of her bouquet, the pair headed for the honeymoon suite at the Morningside Inn in quaint nearby Doylestown. The following morning, they'd catch a flight to a deserted white-sand beach off the gulf coast of Mexico.

Arriving at the inn just before midnight, Grant gathered Nicole up in his arms, carrying her over the threshold. "Welcome, Mrs. Henderson," he said, bestowing a kiss. Flowers, champagne on ice, and a tray of hors d'oeuvres greeted them. The covers on the king-size four-poster bed were freshly turned down. Grant built a fire in the fireplace, turned out all the lights in the room, and opened the champagne.

The warm glow of fire danced in Grant's eyes. He lingered over his kisses for his new wife. Each one grew longer and more intense. No matter how many times they had come to the precipice of this moment, they had never crossed it. Excitement and nerves pricked at Nicole. Grant took the lead. Holding her constant in his eyes, he softly traced the features of her face with his fingers. Releasing her tresses, he let them fall in a cascade down her back. Grant nuzzled the base of her ear, lightly nibbling, working his mouth back to hers. Their breaths had escalated to little gasps by the time his mouth closed over hers. Sliding down the zipper on her dress, they let it glide off onto the floor. Deftly, Grant's fingers moved across Nic's chest down her cleavage, spreading warmth and awareness through her body. Running his hand down her arm, he took her hand and pressed it to him, *there*. Her eyes grew wide. Pulling off his shirt, the firelight flashed in the gold medallion she had given him. His mouth found hers again. Lowering her to the bed, their two feverish bodies melded together into one.

CHAPTER 5

On to Happily Ever After

G rant and Nicole returned from their honeymoon tanned, relaxed, and ready for the Merseymen's New Year's Eve opening night concert in Paris. To their amazement, not one paper—not even the tabloids—had picked up the news of their marriage.

Nicole planned to celebrate their union by burning the wigs and dolly clothes of her alter ego, the model. Gathering up the infernal things, she readied them for a bonfire in the fireplace, when Grant stopped her. "Maybe we should think this one through, luv. Perhaps we're being a bit hasty."

"How do you mean?"

"Through some sort of miracle, our marriage has escaped the press. We have a chance to protect our privacy if we keep this our secret. How bad can that be?"

"How good can it be? They don't know I'm your wife!" she protested. "You told my father you wanted to move the date up so we could be seen together, so we could travel together, so you could kiss me in public. Those reasons don't mean anything now? I'm your wife, and I'm proud of it. I want the world…"

Grant drew her to his side, kissing away her anxious objections. "Of course you're proud of it. But think of it, luv, if the press doesn't know you are my wife, then *you* won't get mobbed. Believe me, I'd feel better about that. Plus, you'll still be able to roam around free and keep the world open for us like you did through the summer and fall. Now Bruce won't have to worry about breaking the news of another Merseyman's wife to the fans. You know the more of us that appear to remain available to the teenybopper birds, the longer we ride our streak. And everyone wins!"

"Everyone, but me." Nic pouted.

"Of course you win. We will still be together for all the important things. See"—he pulled out his wedding medallion from underneath his turtleneck—"we're operating under *your* agreement now. I'll still cuddle you each night in the sack." Grant kissed her, hoping to buy her off.

"But what about all the groupies, all the real dollies that mob you? Will I still have to put up with that?"

Grant interrupted her with an aggressively passionate kiss. "You let me take care of the dollies, okay? Besides," he panted, "I have something else more pressing in mind."

Bruce squirmed at Grant's idea, but he couldn't deny the appeal of not having to wave another wife in the face of the teen-scene fans. Nicole felt cheated but in the end acquiesced for the good of the "whole." At Grant's prodding, they removed their wedding rings and stored them in the bank vault. The birthstone ring went back on her right hand. To add validity to the charade, Bruce moved Nicole out of the flat she and Grant had shared for only thirty-six hours and moved her into a place of her own. True, her new flat backed up to his, and they opened a secret passage between the two places, but it tweaked her nose that Grant had manipulated the situation so that publicly they lived separately.

On New Year's Eve, the Merseymen hit Paris, their second sweep through the Continent in two years. The group received a returning heroes' welcome. Thousands lined the streets from the airport to kick off their '65 tour.

Closing off the streets around the Arc de Triomphe, the officials transformed the plaza into a mega street party. The Merseymen performed on a stage erected underneath the Arc. In a platinum wig and a gear leather mini, Nic joined the almost fifty thousand pulsating rockers who swelled the streets that night. The City of Lights bathed them in its radiance. It emanated from everywhere. The Merseymen closed their two-hour concert at midnight as the sky erupted in a barrage of New Year's fireworks. A swell of the choruses from the "Marseillaise" spontaneously rose up as a partisan paraded a huge French flag through the crowd. Swaying, the throng sang along with the national anthem. Free-flowing wine kept the masses warm.

Hungry for more Merseymen, the crowd brought them back onstage following the midnight celebration. As the love from the audience flowed to them, the Boys returned the warmth in number after number. The group played everything they knew, even resurrecting some relics from the old cellar days. Finally at about half past two, the multitude let them go. The four-hour emotional exchange both sated and depleted the group, leaving them physically drained. They had to be helped down the stage stairs. Exhausted, Grant draped his hot, sweaty body over Nic. Ben, George, even Bruce, had to help get all of them into the waiting limousines.

Ironically, the morning following the triumph of Paris, a picture of Grant and the dolly Nicole landed on the front page of the tabloid the *Reflection*. Under the image of Nic helping Grant offstage, the headline splashed, "Paris Mob Mauls Merseymen in Love Fest!" The reporter relegated Nicole's role to that of a "lucky groupie destined to be the latest one-night stand."

Wounded at being lumped in with the despicable gaggle called groupies, Nicole memorized the writer's name, Karl Nielson. "They can't do this to me!" she protested.

Grant merely shrugged. "They can do anything they want."

"But I'm not a groupie."

"Now how would they know that since you decided not to reveal our actual relationship? If you hang around us in public, this is what they'll print. Get used to it." He dismissed her out of hand, as sharply as a slap in the face.

Likewise, Nicole's appeals to Bruce fell on deaf ears. "Let me ring up the reporter and correct the misinformation."

"And tell him what?"

"I can tell him… I'm just a friend of the group…in to help out… I… I…" Nic fumbled for a plausible explanation of her presence.

Bruce detailed for her the facts of life about the press. "Reporters are evil-minded idiots. They write whatever bloody well pleases them and sells the most papers—to hell with the truth. A star, or wife of a star, trades press, even bad press, for keeping the celebrity's name before the public. I don't like it. It stinks. But it's the system, chiseled in granite, held over from the dark ages."

"But can't we do something?" she doggedly kept up.

"Ya, drop it!" he plainly ordered.

And on and on the tour went, across the face of Europe. For the Merseymen, only the decor in the hotel rooms changed. The crowds swarmed, screamed, and swooned the same at every venue. There was no way for them to distinguish a difference. They used their sense of humor and good-natured cheekiness to keep the routine novel.

Despite the captivity, life on tour was heady stuff within that prestigious on-the-road fraternity! Since British groups dominated the charts, while schlepping between cities, the Merseymen's schedule frequently dovetailed with those of the Beatles, the Stones, the Animals—all the top names. Of course, everyone knew each other from the Liverpool cellar clubs, which created an incredible bond. The grapevine kept everyone informed about locations and options. Other groups often caught the Merseymen's concert from backstage. Sometimes as a tension reliever, they'd steal into some out-of-the-way club to get in a few riffs with the other touring groups. Other times, they'd rendezvous in one or the other's hotel suite to swap road stories and throw down a few. The Merseymen devised a game they played during these visits—a "spitting contest" of sorts. They each tried to see how outrageous a scenario they could create for the visitors, all the time trying to act as if nothing unusual had occurred. Alcohol increased their bravado. Tall tales and legends grew out of those episodes.

Mid-March the tour wrapped, and Bruce herded the group back to their London studio to lay down more tracks. Recording sessions for the Merseymen dragged on endlessly. Jack wasn't satisfied until every note reflected their sound. They slaved over sections in an unending string of playbacks and re-tapings. Eventually, the tedious repetition wore on Nicole. After one especially grueling afternoon, the group had headed out for what she thought was a cigarette break to clear their heads.

Alone, killing time amusing herself, Nic picked up Jack's headset. Amazed to find it live with a playback, she stepped to the mic. In her wildest dreams, she never figured the mic to be live too. Without hesitation, she sang harmony to Jack's lead, coming through the headphones. Invigorated by the experience, Nic reached back during the musical interlude for Richie's tambourine and used it to accompany the music. Resuming singing—harmonizing more with the lead—she finally concluded in a full-on duet with Jack's taped voice. With the fade-out, she stepped back and bowed to receive her phantom applause.

In actuality, the guys had filed into the booth for a conference with Ben and Bruce about a particularly rough section. With her back to the glass, she never saw them. To her horror, the speaker of the intercom opened, and the ovation for her singing debut was all too real. Whistles, hoots, bravos met her red-faced shame. Puddling into the nearest chair, Nicole buried her face in her hands. Excitedly, the occupants of the booth poured out into the studio.

Pete reached her first, pulling the mortified Nicole to her feet. "That was bloody good! What are ya cryin' for?"

"Yeah! Fab!" Richie hugged her. "You can sing!"

"Hey, yer eyes are leakin'," Jack teased. "Want to stop before yer ruin their fine carpeting in here!"

"Seriously, don't ya know, yer version worked," Pete assessed her performance.

His review caught Jack's attention. "Yeah! It was a gear way to cover the potty part we had. Let me hear it again."

Wiping away her tears, Nic sang it again.

"Now try it like this," Pete encouraged.

"Fab!" Jack lauded, then picked up his section again, forming a duet with her.

"Okay then," Pete picked up. "Nicole, get another pair of head-phones. We'll take it from—"

"Hold on! *What* are you thinking?" Bruce loudly cut in. "It sounds to me like you want Nicole to sing on the record."

"Killer idea, don't ya think?" Richie jumped in.

"No! I don't!" Bruce shouted.

"But it's good. She's good. What's the problem?" Pete lobbied.

"Okay. Show me where it says 'The Merseymen and *a bleedin' girl*.' You think another wife messes us up with the teen-beat set, then try adding a girl to the group. Might as well pull the plug on yer careers now. Where in the damned press releases, the records, or any of the publicity does it say that!" demanded Bruce.

"But...but..." Pete's protest collapsed.

"He's right, you know," Jack said defeatedly.

Bruce prevailed; the Merseymen acceded to his managerial acumen. On the final release, Pete sang Nicole's version of the harmony.

Of all the guys, only Grant remained in the booth that day, stabbed in place by Nicole's undeniable talent. Her boldness embarrassed him. His gut-level resentment and jealousy of his wife confused him.

Although Mary didn't witness Nicole's little studio escapade, her student related it to her ally blow by excruciating blow, when Mary showed up for studies that evening while the group was out for costume fittings. Unable to do more than listen, Mary didn't possess the magic elixir to soothe Nicole.

However, Nicole's first singing effort hadn't gone up in smoke; Ben had recorded it. Late that evening, Ben and Bruce stopped by Nicole's London flat. Still smarting from the sting of her antic at the mic, she reluctantly let them inside.

Bruce, with business on his mind, entered efficiently. "Nicole, we need to talk," he started, ushering her toward the living room couch.

Producing a portable tape player, Ben set it up on the coffee table where Mary had cleared a spot.

Bruce slid in a tape. "Listen to this." Out came Nicole's voice. At the tape's conclusion, Bruce exclaimed, "That is marvelous! It's bleeding amazing! I love what I hear! And what I hear is worth millions." Then he looked at her directly. "But you've got to understand, even if I wanted you on the record, I can't introduce you into the group from thin air. The Boys have never even had backup singers on their records. It has to be worked in. Groundwork has to be laid before such a step can be taken. This all has possibilities, but we must proceed with caution."

Hearing her voice on the tape refreshed Nic's embarrassment. Her revived humiliation defeated her ability to comprehend Bruce's meaning. Meekly, she bowed her head. "I'm really sorry. I'll never let it happen again." Involuntarily, her lip quivered.

Realizing her confusion, Bruce picked up her hands in a proprietary fashion and smoothed them in his. "I'm not sorry, Nicole. If you hadn't been so bold, I might never have found such a wonderful new talent. It's just going to take me time to figure out how or if I should incorporate you with the Boys or start you out on your own." He raised his eyebrows in a smile of encouragement.

"What?" She blinked blankly back at him.

"I want to sign you. You're damn good, and I want to be your agent. You've got a future." His smile echoed encouragement.

"You want to sign me?"

"Yeah. If you say yes, I have the papers here."

Nicole looked to Ben's direction, seeking his confirmation. Proudly, he beamed.

"Do any of the others know yet?" she questioned.

"No. I needed your okay first. Then I will have conversations with them. We will have to decide if we want to introduce backup singers or another member. Since it is a decision which will materially affect all of them, the decision is theirs. It has to be unanimous and enthusiastic. Why don't you let me handle all the details? Besides, I may just want to start you out on a solo career of your own first."

"What will Grant say?"

Bruce rose to depart. "Leave Grant and the rest of 'em to me. I'll break the news to him." He paused, then closed the deal. "Then you'll sign with me?"

51

"Of course!" she declared, spontaneously coming to her feet. Taking his pen, her hand trembled with excitement. She signed her name where Bruce showed her.

Tucking the tape recorder under his arm, Ben hugged his sister then patted Nic on the back and kissed her cheek as they walked to the door.

Before opening the door, Bruce cautioned her, "Remember, not a word to anyone until I have spoken to them and to Grant."

Uncharacteristically, Bruce touched her cheek. "Be ready, my dear."

Closing the door behind them, Nicole leaned up against it. "*My* career. Mary, did you hear? My career!" she repeated over and over. "The biggest news of my life, and I can't share it with *anyone*, especially Grant!"

CHAPTER 6

Nikki

Days crawled across the calendar as Nicole waited with prickly impatience. Enmeshed in preproduction details of the group's second movie, after two weeks, Bruce still hadn't phoned. The Merseymen's workday stretched to eighteen hours. Routinely, Grant came home far later than anticipated; sometimes he didn't make it to her apartment at all.

To keep herself occupied, Nicole pushed the length of her day to match theirs. Working ahead in her class schedule, by April 1, she passed all her senior-year exams.

Nicole attended the first day of actual shooting on April 4. The director, Graham Wannaker, a wiry, creative type with a short ponytail, ran the concert scenes first. Fifteen hundred lucky fan club members packed the concert hall as extras to play the role of the delirious audience. The Merseymen worked hard to lip-sync the songs exactly as on the master tape, struggling against the urge to embellish or ad-lib. They knew anything extraneous meant hours back in the studio getting the looping right. After five hours, Wannaker cut the extras loose, then shot close-ups and cutaways for an additional three hours.

Amid the remains of the set, at the wrap of the first day's shoot, cast and crew assembled around a small feast the producer, Sam Rottenberg, had catered. Sam, a small, squat Jewish man, with a tanned head crowned by a ring of white hair, loved cigars.

Champagne corks popped as Sam proposed a toast to what he hoped was the start of a successful film.

Following the initial toast, Graham Wannaker stepped to the center of the gathering for announcements. "This certainly has been a productive first day."

The group sent up a round of applause.

"If everything goes this well, I predict a smashing success!" Wannaker played to his group of insiders—building morale, creating a cohesive team. Applause and whistles of enthusiasm erupted.

"Thank you. Thank you. But on a more somber note, as you know, we signed Jane Asher to play the part of the Angel Pauline, who rescues the Merseymen from their date with death. Unfortunately, she's been sidelined with pneumonia and won't be available."

A small moan escaped the mass.

Standing on the outer fringe with Bruce and Ben, Nic paid scant attention to all the hoopla. Hanging out waiting for Grant, she just wanted him to get done with work so they could go home.

"But this won't delay production," Director Wannaker continued. "We've issued a casting call. And I am happy to announce, we found our replacement."

Immediately, a hush of anticipation fell over the group.

"Nicole Moore, would you come up here. Nicole? Where's Nicole?"

A burst of applause broke out.

Nic casually swiveled her head, thinking she heard someone calling her name.

"Nicole Moore, are you here?" Wannaker called out again.

"Ni-cole! Ni-cole!" the crowd started to chant.

Stunned, not realizing what was going on, she threw a puzzled look around the room. Bruce and Ben each grabbed an elbow and ushered her forward through the throng. As the sea parted, there stood Pete, Jack, Richie, and Grant, alongside the producer and director, clapping.

With his hand outstretched to her, Graham started again. "Here's our new angel... Nicole Moore!"

Turning her around to face the group, Graham Wannaker raised her right arm, like a prizefighter after a victory. The applause bolstered by shouts of acclaim swelled.

As the realization dawned on Nicole, she covered her agape mouth.

"As you can see, she's a little amazed," Wannaker explained. "I'm sorry, Nicole, to do this to you; but the guys here wanted to surprise you... A toast to our new Angel Pauline! To Nicole! Hear! Hear!"

Glasses raised. Nicole bowed and accepted the toast.

A stagehand stuck a glass of champagne in her hand. As Nicole sipped from her glass, over the rim, her eye caught Bruce standing off to the side. Apart and alone, he quietly lifted his glass to her and mouthed, "Congratulations."

Finally in the quiet of midnight, Nicole got to discuss the prospect of her career with Grant. He overwhelmed her with his support. In fact, Grant confessed he had suggested her for the part of Pauline. "Oh, luv, we can share everything together now. Pete even wrote you a song for yer part in the movie. It's a love song, and you'll get to sing it to me. See, so now you'll be a part of the music too!"

In between laying out their future, Grant meted out tender kisses. Love warmed his soft brown eyes. "Bruce is going to build you as an entity of your own. If the fans 'buy' you, then it will be natural to add you to our group. Pending fan approval, we'll phase you in. Bruce has it all worked out just like Cinderella. He'll tell the press he went to visit an old schoolmate, heard you singing in the kitchen, and bingo bango, he had to sign you! Once the kids discover you, they'll fall in love with you. They'll feel you're a natural for the movie—then us!"

Grant paused. "There's only one hitch, luv. Since the world doesn't know we're married, and since now the plan has the fans discovering you—clamoring for you—you can't be seen as already being on the inside. For now, we need to live completely apart."

"Well, here's a news flash—we already do!" Nicole dug in.

"No, I mean you'll have to move to another section of town. Once you get the part of Angel Pauline, those louts in the press will see the setup if you live behind me. And it will spoil the next part."

"What next part?" Nic held her breath, waiting for another bomb to drop.

"Our PR people will paint me as a lonely eligible bachelor, desperately seeking the right bird to spend my life with. Eventually, inevitably, me and the new songbird of the movie will be drawn together. Zingo, we become Mr. and Mrs. Happily Ever After!" A huge smile of enlightenment filled Grant's face.

Nicole wasn't smiling.

"It's perfect, don't y'know," Grant pushed.

"I'm not so sure. I don't like the deception, and I don't like being separated from—"

"Hey, luvy, I'm not really going to be goin' out with all those birds. It'll only be for the cameras. When we can, you know I'll bring me home in the rack to you." A lusty leer glinted in Grant's eyes.

Nic didn't want to get sidetracked by Grant's convenient sexual appetite. "I'm beginning to think my having a singing career now is a mistake. Let's scrap the plans, tell the world we are married, and get on with our lives together."

On a dime, Grant soured. "Hey, lady, you're the one who *had to* pick up the mic and sing the other day. This is for you. This is what you wanted. You started this bunch of rot. You'll finish it. Understand? This is the way it is written."

Nicole conformed, believing she only temporarily traded her marriage in the public eye for the start of her career. Other than being repugnant, the plan seemed feasible. Grant left it to Nic to inform both sets of parents—no need for him to throw them into a tizzy. Bruce's sources found her another place eleven kilometers away and moved her during the wee hours of the next morning. Nicole asked Mary to stay in with her awhile to help take the edge off her separation from Grant.

Because of the tremendous success of the Merseymen, Bruce Eckstein's name commanded almost as much respect as theirs did. Any new talent of his garnered the media's maximum attention. Bruce called a press conference to introduce his latest sensation and to hype the imminent release of Nicole's song from the movie as a single. Masterfully before the press conference, Bruce crafted in the press his rags-to-riches story of his new star, teasing her to them. Of course the entire Cinderella saga would be played out soap-opera style, in installments before the media. If executed correctly, the outcry of the fans and the frenzy of the media would feed off each other, advancing each segment and creating the force driving the story. Bruce called this technique "no-hands media manipulation." Nic became the latest "property" to be engendered by his technique. Plus, her career launch became a free prerelease teaser to spike the Merseymen's new movie.

For the press conference, Bruce downsized everything. He and Nicole sat at a modest table in the front of a little room crowded with a limited number of chairs. He knew the chairs would fill instantly with the hounds of the media, all jockeying for position. The agitation of being sardined into the room would create the illusion of white-hot excitement.

Bruce coached Nicole thoroughly. "Project humility and surprise. Remember, less is always more. Let them delight in prying it out of you. Make eye contact, but don't confront. Play to them. Be sincere. Above all, have *fun*."

A hundred ravenous reporters showed up. The room sweltered under the bright-white lights. Popping flashbulbs blinded Nic. Born of nerves, her reaction came from her heart. In a lightning volley, the press fired their questions at her. With energy and captivating assurance, she deftly fielded every one of them.

After a half hour, Bruce shut the show down, leaving the press hungry for more.

To review Nicole's press performance, Bruce had a tiny camera installed in the room to record the event. That evening, a small group, including the Merseymen, came together in the screening room of the film studio, where Wannaker and Rottenberg had just finished scanning the dailies from the day's shoot. Wannaker had the tape of the press conference queued up for them. He hired Nic cold, without ever screen-testing her, because Bruce had arm-twisted her way into the part of Pauline, by trading on the Merseymen's fabulous appeal. Now, Wannaker wanted to see what he bought, how the camera treated her, and how she handled an audience; so he stayed for the screening too. Everyone, but Nicole, sat forward with anticipation in their seats as the tape rolled.

The good-natured joking between the attendees ceased with the appearance of Bruce and Nic on the screen. In stunned silence, everyone watched the thirty-one minutes of black-and-white images flicker through the projector's gate. Finally, the lights came up.

Breaking the spell, Graham stopped long enough to pat Bruce's shoulder on his way to the exit. "Wow…what can I say, you dog! You picked yourself a natural." An envious grin crossed his face as he shook his head. "Wow!" He tossed hearty goodbyes at the rest on his way out of the room.

The guys gathered 'round Nicole. Jack led off. "Hey, Bruce, can we just elect her the bleedin' queen now?"

Richie echoed, "Yeah, Grant. You can just sit back and retire. Let yer little bird bring home the bacon."

Jack chirped, "Queen of hearts, queen of hearts!"

"Might as well." Grant lobbed a friendly arm about Nic's shoulder. "Ain't she just got it all!"

"Ya know we can't just call you Nicoooooole… Moooooore," Pete said, obviously dragging out the *o*'s in her name. "It doesn't fit that bird." He pointed toward the blank screen. "Ya need somethin' more, somethin' lively, somethin' kicky." Pete paused and thought. "Hey, that's it! Kicky Nicky! We'll call you Nicky."

"Nicky? Nicky Moore?" the star-to-be questioned.

Bruce mouthed the name over and over to himself. "No. Nikki, N-I-K-K-I. Just Nikki. Like Elvis is just Elvis. No last name. Nikki." From that moment on, to almost everyone in the world, she became Nikki—the indomitable Nikki.

With gusto, Bruce seized on launching her career. The tape of the press conference confirmed he chose a moneymaker. From the screening room, they raced to the recording studio. Bruce wanted a turnaround of one week on her new single.

"Nikki, the clock is ticking!" Bruce exhorted her. "Every hour, of every day, of the first few weeks is the most critical. A once-and-done press conference without production accomplishes nothing, even from me. I want the press lapping at your heels. You'll have to keep up! It's the constant barrage in the media that keeps the excitement alive. Without excitement, you're yesterday's news. Every album requires a tour and a special if it can be arranged. The more we push, the more we get. And we need to push as hard as we can without oversaturating the market. *We* create the appetite, then almost satisfy it. Always leave them wanting *more!*"

Pressure mounted on all of them to produce—and on schedule. Sitting with bleary eyes at four in the morning listening to final playbacks became normal for her. Studio life morphed into an infinite series of hurry-ups and waits. In between takes, Nikki dined on bites of greasy, cold, congealed fish and chips, washed down with sips of warm, flat Pepsi. But none of the inconveniences mattered when she stood in front of that microphone and recorded the music that filled her soul. Her balloon never landed. She greeted each day with a smile that started inside her heart. The "holy-gee-whiz!" feeling bursting inside her couldn't be quelled.

In conjunction with the print media, Bruce lined up three UK TV dance-party shows to introduce Nikki's single. By the end of the first week, a little horde of reporters camped out during the day on the street below her flat. With each passing day of the successful publicity campaign, their number grew. She debuted at number 25 on the chart. By week 2, she moved into the number 9 position, within striking distance of the Merseymen's number 1 spot. That feat reaped considerable attention from Grant. Nikki passed from anonymity to notoriety in less than a week.

Simultaneously, Nikki caught on, on the Continent. Bruce scheduled appearances for her in France, Germany, Italy, and Spain over the following three weeks. Paparazzi now dogged her everywhere, reducing contact between Nic and Grant to almost zilch.

Grant complained bitterly to her over the phone. However, nightly the press snapped photos of his arm hooked around a different dolly.

Meanwhile, the Merseymen continued to skyrocket off the US charts. Because Bruce feared tinkering with their success in the extremely lucrative and supremely fickle American market, he limited Nikki's initial release to the European and East Asian continents.

Even though she had spent a great deal of time with the group, Nikki remained naive about the relationship between a manager and a personality. Violating a fundamental rule, Nikki had Mary deliver a note to the reporter from the *Reflection* who had caused her so much grief. Following one of Bruce's many-choreographed photo ops with the press, Mary sought out Karl Nielson, requesting a private meeting with Nikki at the Brass Rail Café.

With only two patrons in the café, Nikki didn't have any trouble picking out the reporter. For sure he wasn't the impeccably dressed blond. He had to be the one in the loosened tie, rolled-up shirtsleeves, and no jacket. She went in with her hand extended in introduction. "Mr. Nielson—?"

"Karl," he interrupted as he pulled out a chair for her.

"Thank you. I need to talk to you confidentially—"

"Off the record," he interrupted.

"Off the record?" Nikki questioned.

"Yeah. If you want to talk to a reporter and not have him write about it, you need to say 'off the record.' Then he puts down his pen, and he's ethically bound not to report it."

"Okay. I want to talk to you off the record."

Nielson shot glances around the room. Satisfied, he capped his pen then closed his notebook on the table. "Okay. I'm listening."

"Worried?" she quizzed him.

"No, just cautious. You're hot cargo. I wanted to make sure none of my competitors are within earshot... So what's so important?"

"Mr. Nielson... Karl, off the record, what do I have to do to get around the innuendo and downright lies in your paper?"

"Give us a story to print."

Ignoring his comment, Nikki continued on with her agenda. "Like in Paris this past January, you referred to me merely as 'a lucky groupie destined to be the latest one-night stand.' How do I stop that?"

"Give me the real story to print."

"But…that's it?" she questioned, floored by the simplicity of his request.

"Yep. In the absence of news, we make up whatever fits the picture of the day. Celebrities, and splashy headlines about them, sell papers. We have a quota of pages to fill each deadline. If my paper sells, I eat. If my paper sells really well, I eat better. If you won't talk to us, then what's left for us to write? We connect the dots the best we can. Stories have to come from somewhere. But that's off the record, and you can't quote me on that." His eyes twinkled.

"But there's the press conferences and—"

"Oh, please! Those are so scripted. We show up for the gaffes." He paused, for a millisecond of thought, then pounced. "Aha! See, if you were in Paris, then you *have* met the Merseymen already!"

Caught in his snare, Nikki's eyes widened in fear. Coolly, she came back to cover her panic. "But this is off the record."

Karl threw his head back in laughter. "Don't worry, Princess. I won't blow your pat little PR story. I know how this game works. I know that if I let the cat out of the bag, I'll be cut off—"

Nikki interrupted, "Karl, what if I called you with stories? Or if you had my number and you called me with questions?"

It was Karl's turn for wide-eyed amazement. "You mean you'd give me a lead?"

"Better than a lead, I'll give you stories, real stories. If you have a picture, call me. I'll explain it or give you the off-the-record low-down."

"You'd do this for me?" Karl asked incredulously.

"Not just for you. See, Karl, that's the problem. What about all the other papers? How can I handle all of them? Could you be a conduit to them too?"

"Like a press agent?"

"No. Just a well-placed leak, I mean source. You'll get all the calls first. In return for the inside scoop, you'd run interference for me—let me know about any dirt about to appear somewhere else."

"Lady, I like your style." He wagged his head in admiration.

"Maybe if you had the actual stories, we won't get smeared so much. You understand I can't speak for—" Nikki caught herself before she blurted out too much.

"Go ahead, we're off the record."

"Do you promise?" Realizing she was on shaky territory, she lowered her voice. "The stories right now are only about me. I can't speak for anyone else."

"Why? Who else would you be speaking for?"

Cornered, she stalled.

Karl leaned in. "You're in with them right now, aren't you?"

"Karl! I can't say any more. I'm already over the line here."

"Aren't you?" he challenged, fixing her in his steely gaze.

"Karl, I'll give you an exclusive—the complete story—but it has to be on my terms, *my* timeline. You can't release it until I say when, no matter what. Understand?"

"Princess, you have a deal." He extended his right hand to seal the pact.

But Nikki held back her hand from wrapping up the deal. "If you get wind of something touchy and I ask, will you deep-six it for me?" She pushed a little further.

"The truth...are you expecting anything?" Karl questioned.

"Honestly, no. But you never know what might pop up." Then Nikki extended her hand. "Deal?"

"Deal!" he said quickly. And they shook.

Gears turned as Karl mulled over possibilities. "You were in Germany too. Dancing...and kissing."

Lowering her eyes, putting a finger to her lips, Nikki nodded with a seductively beguiling smile. "Off the record."

Admiration crept onto his face. He wagged his head. "Lady. Lady. Lady."

Nikki had no way of knowing the dramatic consequences that meeting, in that café, on that day, would ultimately have on the rest of her life. And it had nothing to do with Karl and publicity.

CHAPTER 7

★

Riding the Whirlwind

In week 3 of its release, Nikki's single scored the coveted number 1 spot on the charts, knocking the Boys to number 2. The weeks until her call to be on the movie set flew by. While she made the rounds of the various dance-party shows, the Merseymen began their movie location work in Austria. Bruce practically moved her into the recording studio in putting together her first album. Pete and Jack supplied her with two original songs. The rest of her material Nikki selected from a clearinghouse for songwriters. Ben arranged them; she cut them. On April 28, 1965, Nikki's first album, *Nikki—On the Record*, went into pressing.

Bruce pulled out all the stops to grab attention for his new star. Nikki's first album cover sent shock waves rippling. It featured her standing amid disheveled stacks of newspapers, wearing only a man's white shirt, cuffs undone, with the tails riding high on her thigh. A fedora with a press pass sticking out of the hatband sat askew on her long very tussled tresses. Seductively, the photographer posed Nikki toying with a pencil by her mouth. The flood of controversy produced Bruce's desired publicity coup. Inside a week, the album went gold.

Grant recoiled with objections to the cover, but Nikki merely pointed to his latest dolly pictures in the gossip rags, ending the discussion. Despite the setbacks living separately caused, Nikki remained thoroughly devoted to her Prince Charming Grant. And Grant jealously guarded the naiveté of his little treasure, keeping the seamier side of the business from her, such as the multitudes of "vities" that energized them through the days following their long nights. Occasionally, he'd send one of his lackeys out for a stuffed animal to surprise her, or he'd arrange an intimate rendezvous for them as time and distance permitted. Within their private group, one might catch him grabbing her hand, petting her affectionately, or hanging kisses on her. But just as likely, Grant's moods pivoted; and he'd squander precious moments of their privacy, ignoring her.

Within the phenomenal twirl of Nikki's new life and her advancing career, she kept her recently minted press relationship with Karl Neilson a secret from Bruce. Primed with a draft of an exclusive of behind-the-scenes details that she had given to Karl, Nikki presented it to Bruce as a surprise thank-you present for launching her career. It surprised him—right into a conniption fit.

"Cute," Bruce cynically retorted. "But who released *this* to the night crawlers at the *Reflection?*"

Proudly, Nikki drew herself up to accept Bruce's praise. "I did! I talked to Karl, *that* reporter, about stopping any negative publicity. I gave him the *whole story* as a point of reference—of course it was all 'off the—"

Bruce's exploding fury squashed her. "You did *what?* How could you without asking me first? What have you done? How do you know he won't blow our story line? What assurances did he give you he wouldn't embellish your story with his own brand of facts? He could turn on you and sink you. And take the rest of us down with you!"

Bruce sure twisted Nikki's good news inside out with his sour milk of human nastiness. Not ready to accept his version of press relations, she defended herself. "What's the point of killing the goose who keeps you in eggs? I'll feed him the truth to fill his pages. My system keeps my name on front page and gives us some control over the image. It could work! Armed with the straight dope, he could run interference for us with the other news sources."

"Why have me as your manager? You've already taken this entirely out of my hands. No matter what, I can't undo what you've done. I hope your decision works out for you." Shaking his finger in her face, he warned, "Remember your boundaries. The stories you give concern *you* and you alone. Don't drag the group into your fiasco!"

But before long, Bruce recognized the merits in Nikki's revolutionary idea of press relations and embraced them. At Nikki's suggestion, Bruce pulled Mary into the mix to become her publicist. Soon after, the three of them huddled with Karl Neilson to forge an official relationship. Karl insisted Bruce's incarnation of *Pygmalion* deserved a title. Consequently, he dubbed Nikki "the Princess," a moniker the press and her public enthusiastically adopted. In addition to exclusives, Mary provided Karl with projected timelines so he could make the scene and not miss the big events when they popped.

A week later, Karl scooped the rest of the media as the *Reflection* announced, "Nikki Replaces Asher As Angel—Merseymen to Meet the Princess!"

Austria awaited Nikki's arrival with its arms outstretched and a valuable lesson to teach. Obviously, by the size of the crowd at the airport, Karl's story had crossed the channel. Several hundred eager fans with signs showed up to greet *her*. Bruce never anticipated such a welcome so early in her career, but there they were, standing in a roped-off area just off the tarmac.

Exhilarated, at the top of the plane stairs, Nikki enthusiastically waved hello. A round of cheers answered her as the fans pushed through the rope barricade toward the plane stairs.

From the top of the stairs behind Nikki, Mary saw Bruce and Ben standing helplessly by the waiting limo, across the taxiway. Desperate, Ben started through the throng toward Nikki. Understanding their concern, Mary grabbed for Nikki to pull her back and give her a quick lesson in mob mentality. Too late, lithely, Nikki skipped down the stairs into the waiting mass of adoring fans.

Photographers snapped her descent into the mob. Shaking hands, she autographed everything from scraps of paper to the backs of blouses. The spirited body pushed toward her. Oblivious to the danger, Nikki waded in deeper.

From the crowd, a reporter shouted, "How do you like Austria?"

"Beautiful. The people are great!" Nikki threw open her arms.

An enthusiastic hometown cheer swelled up and pressed in to return the embrace.

"Are you excited to meet the Merseymen?"

"Yeah! Wouldn't you be? Don't you think they're kind of cute?" Nikki shouted.

Again, the girls erupted.

Then instead of answering the reporters, now Nikki directed her remarks to the crowd. "What do ya think? Should I tell them you all say hello?"

They squealed. Someone yelled back, "Are you going to go out with one of them?"

"Ooo, do you think I should?"

"Yes. Yes!" And everyone called out the name of their favorite Merseyman.

Clearly, Nikki struck a chord with her audience involvement. She found the power of being able to stir the masses exhilarating. In fact, intoxicating. So she fostered it. "Do you think they'll like me?"

"Yeah!"

"*We* love you!"

"Yeah. Yeah. Yeah!"

"Do you think they'll ask?" She cranked up the level.

"They will. They will!"

"And what should I say?" Nikki hollered.

"Yes! Tell 'em yes."

"You want me to go out with them?" she pushed.

"Do it for us!" someone shouted back.

"Yeah. For us!" the cry went up. They chanted, "Nikki! For us! For us!"

The air sizzled with the electricity of their spontaneous rapport.

White-faced with fear, Ben finally fought his way to Mary's side near Nikki.

The mounting excitement drew the mob in tighter. Closer and closer they pressed. Ben and Mary tried to buttress the crushing tide. The air got thin. Individuals molded into a mass. The mass rose up like a tsunami. The tsunami lunged at them. Scared, Nikki's eyes doubled; now she understood what she had caused.

Like a ray of light, Nikki caught sight of Karl in the morass and made eye contact with a silent but urgent plea for help.

An earsplitting whistle from Karl cut the air, momentarily silencing the throng, giving Mary time to latch on to Nikki. Darting back to the plane's stairs, the girls ran up them out of the mob's reach.

"Okay. Okay!" Mary addressed them, her hands patting the air in a calming motion. "Nikki'll answer all your questions. One at a time. Please be calm. I promise she'll get to everyone."

The group quieted around the steps.

Lowering her voice to a leisurely tone, Nikki stopped fueling the fray as she answered the questions of reporters and populace alike.

By that time, reinforcements had arrived; and together with the police, Ben organized the assemblage for Nikki's descent onto the tarmac and her limousine. Waving her goodbyes from the frame of the limo door, Nikki called out one last time. "Watch the papers. I'll let you know what happens!" Then she slid inside the waiting car and sped off in safety.

After thoroughly upbraiding Nikki for her actions, Bruce lightened a bit. "You know, I think you hit upon something out there today. The fans and the press together, what a combination! You connected out there with the people."

"Yeah. It was like I'm doing this for them," Nikki inserted.

"No doubt about it, they view you as one of them, almost as a surrogate," Karl acknowledged Nikki. "Truly incredible! And they really want you to do this for them."

"Aside from the mob thing—which I understand now—it felt so right. What if I had more talks with the fans?" Nikki nurtured the seeds of an idea.

Bruce tapped his fingers in concentration. "We could arrange 'chats' with small groups of fans and the press, seemingly impromptu. Nikki could ask their opinion, consult with them, seek their advice; and they'd respond for the 'whole.'"

"Then the press would feed her answers to the world! Oh, I like it!" Mary summed up.

"And my paper would *love* it!" Karl added his enthusiasm. "You know, Bruce, the mob at the airport this morning was good news. It means you've hit the mother lode. Nikki already generates interest on her own." Then Karl directed his attention toward Nikki and smiled. "Face it, Princess, you no longer own your life."

"These little chat sessions with the fans sound great." Nikki hesitated. "I love them, and I treasure their devotion, but I'm not sure I want them deciding the course of my life. Minor decisions that we can manipulate are okay. But after that, I want to live my own life."

Karl roared with laughter. "Your own life, Princess? Then you're in the wrong business."

Bruce shrugged. "I don't picture this format for the long term. But it should serve everyone involved nicely through the next few weeks as Nikki meets the Merseymen."

"Quite right," Karl concurred. "Well, Nikki started the ball rolling this morning by inventing the groupie chat. Now I suggest you schedule another one tomorrow after the *big* meeting between Nikki and the Merseymen. I'm sure the kids will have lots to say!"

The historic event of Nikki meeting the Merseymen unfolded according to Bruce's script. As she exited the hotel that morning, an encampment of media pounced on her.

"Nikki, how do you feel?"

"Are you excited?"

"Did you sleep last night?"

"What will you say to them?"

"Who will you pick?"

That question stopped her. "Pick for what?"

"Which of the Merseymen will you go out with?"

Nikki laughed. "That's assuming anyone asks!" Ducking into her car, the media cortège, like eager puppies, followed them to the studio.

The Merseymen were shooting on Soundstage D. At Bruce's request, Wannaker had issued passes for Karl and a small contingent of the media's upper echelon to get the actual photos and story of the meeting. The rest of the pack would be kept at bay by the front gate and summoned for the press conference following the meeting.

Nearing the scene, Nikki began to perspire. "Geez, I think I've got a case of nerves over this thing today."

"Nerves, I like nerves. It adds a touch of realism." Bruce smiled as he led her through the hangar-sized building to the soundstage where the guys were running a scene.

Waiting until the director yelled "cut," Bruce led Nikki past the press, creating a stir. "There's Bruce. That's Nikki. Get ready. This is it." A slight clatter ensued as the press cadre got up and fell in behind the duo.

While makeup and hair people attended to the Merseymen, they clowned on the set, waiting for the next take. How strange it felt for Nikki to be separated from them.

Following Bruce across the line, Nikki glanced back at the press before crossing over. Suspended in time, they hung there—cameras poised. Overwhelmed by the building anticipation, she kicked out her leg in an excited little "here goes nothing" jig. Crazily, they ate it up; shutters up and down the line clicked a thousand times in rapid succession. Karl secretly flashed her a wink.

Stepping Nikki from the shadows of the soundstage into the light of the set, Graham Wannaker made the introductions. "Guys, I'd like you to meet Nikki—our new Angel Pauline." Passing a few words around, they mugged for the cameras as shutters snapped in deafening proportions. The Merseymen's energy turned the photographers' film. Ceremonially, the Merseymen and Nikki reviewed the script and blocked Nikki's first scene. While Jack made cheeky remarks, the three "single" Merseymen pretended to flirt with her. Finally, they adjourned to the room set up for the press conference as Bruce admitted the pack at the front gate.

"Well, what do you think of her?"

"Fantastic." Richie.

"Cute." Grant.

"Groooovy." Pete.

"Reminds me a bit of me sister." Jack.

"Will you enjoy working with Nikki?"

"I dunno. Can she sing?" Pete.

"Does she act too?" Grant.

"Just as long as she doesn't upstage us." Jack.

The guys dominated—after all, this was their domain. Eventually, Nikki elbowed her way in too.

Finally, the inevitable question: "Nikki, would you go out with any of them?"

"I don't know. I haven't even been asked yet."

Pete headed off the next question. "We have to ask our keeper first."

"Yeah. We don't normally do this datin' stuff on our own," Grant quipped.

"You know we turn in early so we can get our beauty sleep." Richie faked a yawn.

While the insanity of the press conference continued, Mary went out to the small band of fans milling around the studio's front gate and selected twenty to come back for a chat with Nikki. Fresh-faced and ready, they bounded into Nikki's private chat, brimming with questions.

"So how'd it go?"

"Great. Really fantastic," Nikki answered.

"What are they like?"

"They're kind of like us, only really witty... What do you think about them?"

The chatters soon grew oblivious of the journalistic intruders. Their arcing enthusiasm infected everyone in the room.

"So do you like them?"

"How could I do anything else?"

"Would you go out with them?"

"Do you think I should?" Nikki handed it back to them.

"Oh yes! Make it Richie. He's sweet."

"No, Pete is the cutest. You should go out with him."

"Maybe Pete is the cutest, but Grant is sincere. He'd treat you the best."

Eventually, the idea surfaced that she should date all three! Their consensus ruled. Concluding with autographs and pictures, Nikki promised to try their suggestion, telling them to watch the papers to see the progress.

The following day, outside the glare of the press, they got on with the real business of shooting the movie. Learning lines, exchanging roguish barbs, murdering scenes, mucking up, Nikki adapted readily. Now as part of the group, Nikki introduced a fresh element to the game.

When they weren't filming, Nikki with the guys sampled the town's nightlife, in front of the press. They photographed her discoing with Richie, singing with Pete, and slow-dancing with Grant. Bruce brought Candy over for Jack so the four boys could be on the town together. They rode the thrill rides at amusement parks, cut up at fests, and danced till dawn at the trendiest nightspots. When Nikki's presence wasn't required on the set, she and Candy shopped the chic boutiques with the press along for the ride.

The fans soon recognized that Grant emerged as the main suitor for Nikki's affections. Pressure from the chatters mounted for them to declare their love. Readily the "m" word—"marriage"—surfaced. Letting the sexual tension build, Bruce delayed their declaration. He wanted Grant to publicly propose to Nikki from atop the surge of fan enthusiasm the night before their walk down the red carpet at the movie's premiere.

Meanwhile, Nikki's presence with the Merseymen became generally accepted. To get reaction to the plan of Nikki singing with the band, Bruce tested its impact on the chat groups. Emphatically, the fans wanted Nikki to sing with the Merseymen. Together they cut a single—overnight "My Side of Heaven" went platinum.

Bruce grew nervous, very nervous. He had never really planned to cross the two careers. The stratospheric recognition of the pairing of the Merseymen and Nikki panicked Bruce. Just the thought of America getting wind of Nikki desperately frightened him. He feared her presence might dampen the "available male" magnetism the three singles in the group exuded. That charisma supported the group's Stateside popularity, and Bruce didn't want anything to queer that supremely valuable and lucrative prize. But Graham Wannaker wanted to work another song into the movie to cash in on the rising tide of *their* popularity. Bruce refused. In a compromise, Wannaker agreed to release two cuts of the movie: the uncut version for world consumption and the North American version, which didn't include Nikki singing with the guys.

Still, Bruce continued to shore up the dike only he perceived as leaking by booking separate summer tours for them. Bruce scheduled a solo European tour for Nikki while the Merseymen did America.

The separate bookings enraged Grant. He walked off the set, then came looking for Nikki. Pulling her out from in front of a live mic at a recording session, he dragged her to the waiting limo. "C'mon," he growled. "If Bruce thinks he can run my life, then let him deal with this!"

"Driver! Take us to the airport!" Grant snapped.

Punching the gas, the chauffeur squealed away from the curb, sending the limo's occupants sprawling.

Grant's abrupt intrusion both angered Nikki and scared her. She preferred to make herself scarce when one of his "moods" erupted. "Where in the hell do you think we're going?" Nikki yelled at him.

"Back to London! I'll be damned if Bruce thinks he's gonna run my life! We're going to the public registry office, and we're going to get married, before God and the *London Times*! That should put the cat among the pigeons! Let him stop *that* news from going around the world!" Picking up the car phone, Grant foisted it on Nikki. "Here! Call your reporter friend Karl. Tell him what we're doing."

Nikki hung up the phone. "What's that going to solve? We're still bound to his commitments for us and those stupid concerts. We'll be apart anyway!"

"He can't run our lives! I want him to stop! I want to be with you!" Grant whimpered.

"I want to be with you too, and he *can* run our lives. He's our manager. I won't have our marriage used as a weapon—one minute you want to follow the 'plan.' The next minute you want to beat Bruce over the head with it. I'll go with you to the registry office for love, not out of spite."

Breaking down, Grant's lips quivered. "I want to be with you. Make him stop. Make him stop." He wept into Nikki's arms, eventually collapsing into her lap.

Being incorporated into Grant's dilemma—once again his inability to handle their highly pressurized life—forced Nikki into action. Operating from her gut, she rang up Jack to get a bead on what really happened. Jack could tell by her tone, she wasn't in the mood for cheeky.

"That was some show yer boy put on here today. We're quite proud of him. I throttled Bruce after Grant left and demanded to know what kind of crap he pulled on you two." Jack lowered his voice. "Is Grant coming back?"

"In a day or two. He's pretty upset and needs some time."

"Take all you need. We've tied 'im up and stuffed 'im in a closet. Don't worry."

"Jack, do me a favor? Untie the lout long enough to arrange for two tickets to London immediately, on the next flight—even if it's a puddle jumper. Don't bother with any explanation. Just have him do it. Then let the limo driver know."

Next, Nikki gave Karl a "heads-up." "This is one of those times we discussed back in the café. Remember? I need you to deep-six anything you hear on this."

Karl promised.

After a long weekend, she returned to Austria with a refreshed and renewed Grant. That Sunday night, a fortified Nikki knocked on Bruce's door.

Their business genius stood before her, a shaken man. His private hell of personal culpability ate him alive. His condition shocked Nikki. The nurturing side of her wanted to reach out to him, but she knew she had to handle business first.

"These are our lives and feelings you are playing with, Bruce. This can't go on." Then Nikki laid out some new ground rules of her own, calmly, coolly. "First, from now on I will have a suite adjoining the guys'. Disguise it any way you like, starting tonight. Second, the concert schedule will need to be rearranged to provide for a four-day visitation between Grant and me every two weeks. We'll do all the concerts. Just shift the schedule to accommodate our rendezvous. And finally, the film opens on November 2. On November 1, we will be 'engaged' and 'married' before the month is out. From this, there will be no deviation."

Nikki's ultimatum dissipated the tension. For a while, unity returned to the team.

Two days later, the producer, Sam Rottenberg, threw a dinner party for the director, Bruce, the Merseymen, and Nikki. He billed it as a farewell to Austria; but clearly Graham, Bruce, and Sam had another item on the agenda. Toward the end of dinner, at Sam's urging, Bruce stood to suggest that the Merseymen and Nikki do a joint concert as a farewell to Austria and another as a welcome concert in England.

Rising in unanimous assent of the idea, with wild enthusiasm, the guys and Nikki abandoned the party to assemble the roster of songs, write a few new ones, and plan for the inevitable accompanying album.

Despite Nikki's records and her lip-syncing dance-party shows, this combination concert would be her first performance in front of a screaming, paying mob of fans. The guys rehearsed her for three days to acquaint her with her parts, the gear, and the stage.

Onstage the night of the performance, nervous anticipation tightened in Nikki's stomach. With the audience before her, shielded from them only by the cool blackness and the common, anxious quiet, her imagination ran rampant. Even though Grant stood next to her, squeezing her hand, Nikki thought she'd throw up!

Then the introduction, "Ladies and gentlemen, THE MERSEYMEN AND NIKKI!" Gulping her final breath, Nikki held it. *Flash*! The heat of the spotlights hit her. Waves of screams and cheers crashed over her, vaporizing her jitters.

Richie counted them down with his sticks, and off they flew. Nikki's confidence surged as she took turns harmonizing with Pete, Grant, and Jack. Stimulated, she boldly removed the mic from the stand, and the guys encouraged her. Dragging the cord behind her, going to the front of the stage, they urged her on. She danced at the edge of the stage, working the crowd, clapping with them. Like proud papas, the Merseymen reveled in her stage presence, grinning from ear to ear. Pete stuck a tambourine in her hands.

When the first of her two solos came around, Nikki took center stage from Jack, belting out her song. Through cavorting with the Merseymen, Nikki discovered the audience's hot buttons that triggered their participation and emotional oneness. Playing to them, she made as much eye contact as possible, and they lapped up all her attention. Too soon the end of the concert came, and nobody wanted to leave. Taking their bows to a thunderous tumult of applause, the audience demanded three encores—the group gave them two. The sweet rush of euphoria after the concert engulfed Nikki, spinning her head. She basked in the concert's afterglow for hours.

Crossing the channel, landing back on their home turf, the London concert crowd went ballistic for the combined effort. Cashing in on their smashing success, Bruce booked them for three additional UK concerts and swung his fabulous music machine into high gear. A lightning round with the cover photographer placed the Merseymen in cardboard cutouts of train cars—Jack in the engine, the rest of the guys spilling out of other cars—with Nikki in a funky chugging-to-keep-up caboose. In two weeks, their collaborative album *The Merseymen with Nikki on Board* hit the streets, going platinum overnight.

Nikki's success didn't eclipse the boys'. Her star soared in conjunction with theirs. The exhilaration of the magic comet ride escalated. The crowds, the glitter, the lights, the applause, all fed the incessant ecstasy. Nikki heard the seductive song of the siren, and her name was Adulation. What a mesmerizing aphrodisiac!

CHAPTER 8

★

Destiny

Bruce brought Nikki's parents over to do a taped interview for Nikki's first TV special and to witness her performance in the last of the combination concerts. Grant couldn't resist introducing her parents to the audience. He drew the crowd's wild and frenzied reaction by kissing his "babe" onstage. Richard and Fran beamed from the front row. Because they lived outside the hype of the European press, the extent of Nikki's popularity and the magnitude of her career astounded them. Several times during the concert, both of them remarked, "Wow, they really like her!" or "Can you believe they're going crazy for our daughter!"

Afterward, an "old home week" reunion of sorts took place backstage as the band welcomed Fran and Richard. After all, Fran, with Nikki, had spent the previous summer touring with the group. To celebrate properly, Bruce suggested they move the party to the film studio since he wanted to review the movie's "dailies" anyway.

Piling into limousines, Fran and Richard rode with Grant and Nikki. Never shy about things on his mind, Richard promptly addressed his issues. "I don't mind telling you both that this business of the two of you living separately distresses us."

In an amazing turn, Grant jumped on his comment. "We're not too terribly fond of it either, thank you. This was not what I had in mind when I asked Nikki to marry me. In fact, her career came as a bit of a bolt from the blue. Heh? Didn't it, *luvy?*" With his mockingly saccharine tone, Grant manufactured *and* opened a can of worms.

Tossing the responsibility of their separation back on Nikki startled her. *What did he mean by that? And where did it come from?* With a shrug of her shoulders and a half smile to her parents, she tried to hide her embarrassment. She knew this brush of friction sliced to the quick of their hearts and would precipitate a serious conversation with them later. But long before that, Nikki determined she would have her own tête-à-tête with Grant Henderson. His remarks aggravated her.

The group arrived just as Graham and Sam had set up the dailies from the movie shoot in the screening room. In between clips, Sam nattered on about his prize production from inside his cloud of blue cigar smoke. By the time they finished in the projection room, a spread of delicacies and a full bar had materialized on the soundstage. Delighted in playing to his intimate audience, Sam kicked off the impromptu party. Squiring Nikki's parents, he proudly acquainted them with the movie business by initiating a personal tour of the studio.

After an hour or so, Grant swaggered up to Nikki, his love of gin and tonic in clear display. A cigar in one hand, his drink in the other, he playfully growled, "C'mere, luv." With his gin-saturated breath, he whispered in her ear, "I know a lonely li'l couch in a dressing room that's lookin' for company." And he slopped a kiss on her neck.

"You do, huh? Well, why don't you show me?" Nikki cajoled, wanting to get him alone for the answers to the salvos he launched in the limo.

Carelessly, he lobbed his hand with the cigar on her shoulder; its smoke wafted up into her face. His drink sloshed in the glass as he clumsily guided Nikki toward his dressing room.

Anger mixed with disgust backed up in her throat.

Closing the door, he locked it behind them. Putting his drink and cigar down on the makeup counter, he wrapped his paws around Nikki, planting a sopping-wet kiss on her mouth.

Nikki wiggled free. "Grant, please wait. We need to talk. I have to ask you something."

"Sure, luv, anything." He leaned against the counter, full of himself, self-assured, swaggering. "Then I have something for you." Crudely, he tugged at his crotch.

Nikki ignored his boast. "I thought you wanted me to have this career. I thought you wanted me to be in the business with you."

He winced slightly in a small effort to recall the conversation. "Ya, so?"

"Then what was that attitude you pulled in the limo with my parents? You didn't sound so gear about this anymore."

Grant snickered disdain. "Well, well, *Princess*, did I embarrass you? Maybe things aren't so perfect in yer li'l world?" He picked up his drink and scowled, raising his voice, "Well, look around ya, luv! Ain't this a sight! When's the last you've been with me in the rack?"

Incredulous, she fought back. "If you remember, *I* wasn't the one who came home with the damned idea of separating. Seems like you proposed it!"

He swigged from his glass. "Yeah, well, no one expected you to take over! No one thought you'd amount to anything. We all thought you'd just stand in the back and hum a li'l bit!"

His comment stung, as if the back of his hand had slapped her across her face. Tears welled up inside. But she'd be damned if he'd see her cry! Pulling herself up, her eyes narrowed. Words came from deep within her throat. "Then why didn't you say so? Why didn't you find your own stupid voice and say so?"

"Well, damn ya to bleedin' hell, Nicole! I thought ya could have at least serviced yer man better!" Grant took his drink, cocked his arm back, and hurled it.

The glass hurtled past her ear and shattered on the brick wall behind her. Ricocheted drops of gin and tonic pricked the back of her legs.

She stepped toward him. "Then I suppose my standing up to Bruce and setting some ground rules for our tour meant nothing! You know what you need to do? You need to decide what the hell you want, Grant Henderson! And maybe we can settle on that! In the meantime, sober up." Turning deliberately, Nikki walked to the door, opened it, and paused. "You're right, Grant, your couch does look lonely. Maybe *you* should keep it company!" She punctuated her exit by sharply closing the door.

The hot sting of tears bit her eyes, then cut rivulets down her cheek. Grant's words sliced deep. *Do the rest of the guys think I'm taking over? Do they really expect me to just stand in the back and hum?* Nikki needed answers fast! In the washroom, she splashed cold water on her face to hide the puffy traces of tears, then dabbed on some more makeup so she could rejoin the party. Nikki wasn't about to let tears betray her or provoke sympathy for her. Walking fast, she picked up a rum and Pepsi from the bar for courage, then politely pulled Jack out of his conversation.

"Well, Princess, what have you and yer boy really been up to?" Jack raised his eyebrows in a brazen leer.

"Jack, please! It's serious."

Instantly, he dropped the pretense. "What's wrong? Is Grant okay?"

"Yeah. Grant's fine. We...we had a fight."

"Is that all?"

"No, Jack, that's not all. Grant said some things I need honest answers to... We fought about my career and my singing with the Merseymen."

"I never would have guessed," Jack retorted sarcastically.

"What do you mean?"

"Just that I saw that coming after Grant's row with Bruce. He won't stand up to Bruce. I figured sooner or later you'd get it. And—"

"Did you and the rest of the guys really think I would just stand in the background and hum a little bit? Have I taken this career thing too far? Do you want me to go away or fade into the background?"

Jack's anger drew him up. "Grant said that? What a fool! What a lolly bleedin' fool!"

Nikki drank in his bitterness.

"That thick son of a bitch! No. Hell no, Nikki. The night Bruce proposed a career for you to us, we ran the entire gamut of possibilities. We each had a voice in the decision—*one* negative and you'd still be a step-'n'-fetch-it today. It was very clear that you could either go on yer own or eventually be teamed with us. We wanted you with us. The vote was four to one. Bruce wanted to keep you solo, but his vote didn't really count. Why do you think Pete and I wrote you those songs? We wanted to cement our partnership and bring you luck. That's why I tore Bruce apart when Grant collapsed a couple of weeks ago. What's he so afraid of in America? We all assumed you'd be coming on the North American tour. Pete and I started workin' up new routines for you."

"Then you're not threatened by my popularity?"

"Are you kidding? To put it bluntly, the ten thousand who came to see you perform in Vienna wasn't exactly the fifty thousand we get. Besides, wouldn't yer success be good for us too? Wouldn't we be sharing the same gate? I don't see yer name solo on that marquee—or even first!"

Jack had been serious about all he could stand. "Hey, you're not part of some *eeevil* plot to take over the Merseymen, are you?"

"Yes!" Nikki prophetically joked. "And you'd better lock up your gold."

With nothing to hide, Nikki rode back with her parents to their hotel where they talked into the wee hours over tea. At four in the morning, Nikki knew the groupies in front of her flat had long ago given up and gone home. But instead of an empty street, the group's limo sat parked out front. Nikki tapped on the window. The driver lowered the glass; it was none other than Jarred, head of the tour's security, at the wheel.

"What's up?" Nikki quizzed.

"He wants to speak to you." Jarred motioned with his thumb. Grant lay sprawled, unconscious in the back seat.

"Okay." Nikki sighed. *Haven't we had enough for one night?*

With a deep breath of resolve, Nikki slid in. Grant stirred to life, reeking of stale gin. "Oh, Nikki. Dear Nikki." Ham-handedly, he patted her hair, whining, "Are you leavin' me?"

"Good night no, Grant. Can't we talk about this later? Why don't you go home and sleep this off?"

His stupor answered as he slumped back in the seat. Nikki had Jarred drive to an obscure hotel outside the city and check the

"Smiths" into adjoining rooms. Then he helped her get Grant into bed.

Grant awoke with seismic activity in his head at noon. After throwing down a few pills, he recovered enough for a quiet supper together. Now they faced each other over dinner in the room.

"Luvy, I don't know what got into me last night," Grant started, then he sniffed a chuckle. "I s'ppose it was too much gin. You know I never mean to hurt ya. Yer all I have in the stupid world. Let's forget it ever happened and just go on. 'Kay?"

Not up for sweeping it under the rug, Nikki pushed for settling it. "Grant, why didn't you ever tell me that you didn't want me in the business with you? Why didn't you confide in me that it bothered you?"

He propped up his head on his hand. "I never thought it did. I'm lonely. I thought you'd be around all the time if you sang with us. But it's not working that way."

"It will. We'll be together until July. America is only six weeks, then we're back together. November we announce our 'engagement' and 'get married.' But I need to know right now if you have a problem with my career. Whether solo or with the guys…is there a problem with me having a singing career? Tell me. I have to know."

He averted his eyes. "No…you're not going to leave me, are you?"

"No, of course not. I made a promise to you. I'm not going anywhere." Walking around behind him, she massaged his neck, then bent down to kiss him. "You know, if you said the word, I'd give it all up tomorrow and just be your wife."

"I know, luv," he answered under his breath. "I know."

The five weeks before their separate tours drove Nikki and the Merseymen hard. Bad weather and Grant's mood swings put the movie behind schedule. Meanwhile, in addition to her numerous chat sessions, Nikki cut her second solo album, *Simply Nikki*. Karl's photographer Jimmy captured a stunning solitary portrait of the

Princess onstage before the microphone in a rainbow of stage light for the album cover.

Of course through it all, Grant and Nikki managed time in front of the media acting out their courtship charade.

Before Nikki knew it, the day arrived when a jet waited to whisk her off to Germany for her initial solo appearances. Looking into her makeup mirror that morning, the realization dawned on her for the first time that she would be doing the concerts *alone*! No Grant to squeeze her hand before the lights exploded on; no Pete to flash her encouraging winks or Jack taunting her to go further. No matter how many times everyone tossed around the words "solo" or "on your own," Nikki never really thought about the fact that "they" wouldn't be alongside her. In the nonstop pandemonium of the previous five weeks, she lost the stark reality of those words. Now it all came down to her. For the first time, the responsibility for the entire show rode on her shoulders. Exhaling, she nodded to her image. "Here's to you, kid."

Bruce, Grant, and the rest of the Merseymen congregated at the airport's gate for the final farewell scene. Desperately, Nikki wanted a private moment with Grant. She needed to share a few personal words with him, to look into his soft brown eyes and have them assure her. But once again what should have been private time became fodder for the public press. From behind barricades, a thousand fans waved their goodbyes to her, while trying to catch the attention of the Merseymen.

Likewise, Bruce hurtled startling changes in Mary's direction. Because Bruce wouldn't divide himself between the Merseymen and Nikki, he deputized Mary to handle the managerial chores of Nikki's first tour—a mere six weeks after he had installed her as Nikki's publicist! So as Bruce winged his way to America with the Merseymen, Nikki and Mary settled into their hotel rooms before rehearsals in Hamburg, confessing their apprehensions to each other in one massive, cathartic rant session. Over glasses of sparkling white wine, they decided if Nikki were honest with her fans, they would support her—and all the rest they'd improvise—as they had up to that point.

In the cool blackness before the lights came up, rather than tasting the dread of stage fright, Nikki united herself with the audience, feeling the energy of their anticipation, waiting, building to be spent. Touching their excitement fueled her own. She could hardly wait for the announcer's introduction.

"Ladies and gentlemen, in her first solo performance...the indomitable NIKKI!"

Delirious cheers of their resounding exuberance electrified Nikki. The spotlights ignited her.

"HELLO!" she hailed them. "Thank you for being here! I LOVE YOU!" Then stepping to the mic, she delivered everything they came to hear, and more. Along with Nikki, they clapped, they danced, and they sang along. The audience stretched her hour-and-a-half-long gig to over two hours! Nikki finished to a standing ovation.

She planned for one encore; they *demanded* more.

Coming back for her second encore, out of the corner of her eye, Nikki spotted a stool in the wings backstage. Grabbing it, she brought it onstage with her. Walking to center stage with a mic, she sat down on the stool, then turned her attention to the stage manager behind the wing curtain. "Could you kill all the lights, and could I have just a single spot on me?"

A hush of high expectation fell over the audience. Mary watched the entire staff behind the scenes go into cardiac arrest over Nikki's request.

Then Nikki addressed her band. "Guys, go ahead and take five. I've got this." The band threw nervous looks at each other and at Mary, before filing offstage.

Calmly, Nikki repeated her request. "Please, just a single spot. I'll find it. Okay?"

Silence riveted the audience. In the lone spot from atop a humble stool, Nikki offered them an unvarnished version of herself and, in the process, struck for herself an enduring trademark.

"I can't thank you enough for taking me into your hearts. You'll never know how much your love tonight means to me. I will carry you and this performance with me always. But in your graciousness, you've run me out of songs. If you'd allow me, I'd like to do a couple of love songs for you. I hope their powerful emotions convey the depth of love I feel for you tonight." Bowing her head, without musical accompaniment, Nikki started a cappella "PS I Love You," picked up "Grateful for You," then concluded with a heartfelt rendition of "Take My Heart." Raw emotion fortified her voice. The audience exploded in a tremendous ovation, holding her transfixed with their applause. Bowing and thanking them, she inched her way offstage.

The band, stagehands, and crew swept Nikki up with their enthusiasm. Delirious, the Label's promoters filled the halls. Baskets upon baskets of pink roses overflowed her dressing room—from Bruce, the Merseymen, and all avenues of the trade. Sam Rottenberg showed up to celebrate.

The heady froth of success carried Nikki across Europe. City after city fell before her wave. Reviewers raved. Every show sold out. Even SRO tickets vanished practically before the ink dried. Television and radio stations vied for interview time. Like the Merseymen, she held press conferences before every performance and continued with her informal chat sessions, usually after a concert.

Nikki found that the bimonthly, four-day meetings with Grant interrupted the momentum of her concert series. But she considered them necessary for the health of their marriage and refused to curtail them. The romance of stolen moments in a steamy seaside paradise partially compensated for their separation.

July 19, 1965—her eighteenth birthday—found Nikki in Naples. Following yet another triumphant exit from the stage, a group of promoters and elite press corps congregated around Nikki outside her dressing room door. Momentarily distracted, something drew her attention from the surrounding horde. Like a lone shaft of light piercing a cloudy gray sky, there stood a man, the likes of which Nikki had never seen before. In his early thirties, he emanated conservative class, borne of either nobility or old money. Tall—a little over six feet—he swept his sandy-blond hair off to the right at a rakish angle. A roguish twinkle sparked in his incredibly blue eyes. Exceedingly comfortable in his white dinner jacket and satin striped trousers, his clothes distinguished him as they stood in stark contrast to the trendy-chic getups of the others. Nonchalantly, he leaned one shoulder against the corridor wall, taking in the scene, casting a bemused smile in Nikki's direction. His intense attention penetrated her.

Slightly intimidated by his direct gaze, Nikki cast her eyes down, looking away for a moment. When she looked back up, he had disappeared, as mysteriously as he appeared. Such profound scrutiny baffled her. *Who is he? What does he want?*

CHAPTER 9

★

Humpty Dumpty

November 2, 1965, premiere day, dawned clear and extraordinarily sunny. Successfully, Bruce had convened the three corners of his publicity triangle, creating a superb confluence. He built the sexual tension between Grant and Nikki to a feverish pitch, swelled the rising tide of the Merseymen and Nikki's ever-expanding popularity, and intensified the anticipation for the movie.

Vada Knight costumed them for the premiere. She clothed the Merseymen in long black velvet Edwardian-cut tuxes with oversized four-in-hand ties. Nikki glowed in her golden satin gown with natural waist and dropped shoulders. Grecian curls cascaded down the nape of Nikki's neck with a string of gold sequins entwined through them. For the crowning touch, on her left hand, Grant had borrowed a five-carat diamond solitaire for Nikki to wear. Her actual two-carat engagement ring would be rescued from the bank vault outside the glare of the cameras.

Five limos snaked their way through the crowded streets to the theater. Precise pacing of the cars gave the press at least five minutes of solo face time with each Merseyman on the red carpet. Jack's limo arrived first, followed by Pete's then Richie's.

Grant exited his car to questions about an "impending" engagement. Playing coy, he shyly received his accolade, biding his time waiting for Nikki's limo. When it arrived, he opened the door and offered his hand to assist her. As planned, the diamond ring emerged first, tarrying for a moment in full view of the press. Flashbulbs popped profusely, setting fire to its brilliance. Then Grant pulled Nikki up and beside him. Wrapping his right arm about her shoulder, he waved with his left. They posed together, displaying the ring.

"Congratulations! When's the big day?" the press called out.

"Thanks! What day is that?" Grant impishly threw back.

"When are you getting married?"

"I don't know yet. I have to ask her father," Grant teased.

"When did you ask her?"

"Last night. Got down on me knees and everythin'. What do ya know? She said yes!" Grant raised Nikki's left hand in triumph then drew her into a kiss. The throng erupted in wild cheers.

Inside, red velvet ropes lined off rows for their party. From their special section, Sam and Graham fraternized with assorted studio dignitaries who came to be seen at the premiere.

Taking in the action, Nikki noted a man in a serious black business suit smoothly slip his way through the mass to Sam, Graham, and Bruce, garnering their collective ear. They all nodded, smiled, tossed a look at the group, then back to the man.

"Aha, somethin's afoot," Grant whispered into Nikki's ear. The others also noticed and gathered their heads together to figure out the news.

Beside himself with jubilation, Bruce strode up the aisle to the group. "That was Her Majesty's secretary. The royal family *will* attend the premiere. They've dusted out the royal box and all! Afterwards, Her Majesty desires an audience with you backstage. Her footman will be 'round to instruct us in the correct behavior." Bruce grimaced at the thought of Jack receiving instructions on proper protocol.

For Nikki, the excitement of meeting the royals drowned out the film and even the wild ovation at its conclusion. Over and over in her mind she practiced her curtsy, hoping she wouldn't trip when she executed it.

Uniformed guards escorted them to a secure room backstage where the royal family waited. They stood in a formal reception line, and the honorees queued up in another line to be presented. Jack, Candy, and Jack Junior stood first for introductions. Three-year-old

Jack Junior breached the walls of formality, charming everyone with his version of royal etiquette. Bowing deeply from the waist before the queen, from his bent-over position, he looked up at Her Majesty and said, "Am I doin' this right, ma'am?" Laughter from everyone cut the tension.

"You are doing just fine, young man," replied the queen as she took his little hand and raised his position to normal stance. She bent over slightly so they could speak on more direct terms. "So how old are you, young man?" she queried him.

Jack intervened, "If I might, Your Majesty." Picking Jack Junior up in his arms, he relieved the queen of her uncomfortable stance and allowed them to communicate at eye level.

A House of Windsor photographer snapped pictures of everyone as they met Her Royal Highness—a personal memento of the occasion.

Dashingly, Prince Charles took time for a personal aside to Nikki. "You know, normally I detest pop music, but I find your voice intriguing. I should like to attend one of your concerts."

"I would be deeply honored by your presence, Your Majesty," Nikki responded with a curtsy.

Talk of the royal audience followed them to the hotel ballroom where Sam Rottenberg hosted a lavish premiere party. A larger-than-life-size ice sculpture of the four Merseymen with the title of the film, *Trapped!* etched in huge letters below greeted the guests as they entered. Champagne flowed over the base of the sculpture, forming a fountain of the bubbly. Behind that, sumptuous food heaped to overflowing spilled across a runway of tables. A full-service bar lined one wall, and waiters passed through the partygoers exchanging half-full glasses for brimming ones. The room teemed with power brokers and movie aristocracy. Sam kept the magic and glitter sparkling through the night with a planet-sized mirror ball turning above their heads.

A bit shy to go wandering, Nikki stood at Grant's side as he led her in and out of conversations from one luminary to another, feeling free for the first time publicly to have his arm about her waist. To her utter amazement, again and again legends of the business took their time to compliment her on her performance.

In the course of the evening, Nikki returned to the champagne fountain for a bit more bubbly. Holding her glass under the flow, another glass joined hers. She cast a customary, polite glance up at her fountain companion, only to come face-to-face with that mysterious man she had seen in Naples. His blue eyes danced. The spotlights coaxed strands of rich gold from his perfectly styled hair. His designer tuxedo accentuated his robust frame.

Raising his glass as if in a toast to her, he said, "It would have been a better sculpture had the sculptor carved your figure. But I doubt an earthly artist could capture such perfection." Then turning with a wink, the crowd swallowed him up.

Dawn's first light brought a sampling of the reviews to their hotel suite. Some version of "Merseyman Engages Princess" captured all the bold type. In paper after paper, the picture of Nikki's rock eclipsed the premiere story, relegating it to "below the fold" position.

As time for their official marriage neared, Grant hunted a place for them to live. He eventually settled on a white Georgian manor with a black mansard roof in Surrey. Willows wept gracefully over a gentle stream that burbled through its manicured gardens. A stunning grand curved staircase of rich mahogany swept up to the second story from the black-and-white marble foyer. The well-equipped kitchen, with its banks of painted white wood and leaded-glass cabinets, opened onto a garden room eating area. Walls of French doors lined the room, providing a commanding view of the grounds.

To privately commemorate their anniversary, on December 24, 1965, Grant and Nikki made it official for the world. In the company of Bruce and the Merseymen and with Mary and Candy again at her side, they stood before the public registry in London and said their "I do's." This time news of their marriage flashed across the front page of every major newspaper in the world, including those in America!

Grant carried Nikki across the threshold of the Surrey house where they celebrated their first real Christmas together in the new house with his family and a catered Christmas feast.

Judging by overwhelming fan support for the union of Grant and Nikki, they had no reason to believe that either their relationship or anyone else could torpedo the Merseymen's success. In their naiveté, they scoffed at the fear of change. In his vigilant watch for the enemy from without, Bruce had forgotten about the enemy within.

CHAPTER 10

★

Sitting on a Wall

On January 6, 1966, when they assembled to prepare for their winter tour of South America and the Near East, Richie greeted them with his big news. He and Doreen would be getting married prior to the tour, to be followed by the arrival of their blessed event in June.

Years of being on the merry-go-round of fame began to exact its price on the Merseymen. For eleven years, they had consumed the dream; now it began to consume them. One of the first symptoms of the internal cracking had manifested itself that March of '64 when Grant walked away from the group, when he met Nikki at the lake. The guys handled the mounting repression from years of success's pressure cooker in a variety of ways. Their acid-witted humor lightened the mood, their "vities" kept them on pace, and alcohol relieved the tension of being cooped up. A willing beauty cut from the daily herd of groupies also provided distraction.

No one knew when it happened or the precise cause, but the internal disposition of the Merseymen changed dramatically by the start of their '66 winter tour. The new mood fermenting beneath the surface was so palpable; one could have used the proverbial knife on it. Yet it was invisible, creating the false illusion of normalcy. Restlessness could have been the name of the culprit, that edgy, excitable, jumping-out-of-your-skin, something's-gotta-go-pop feeling.

Of course evolution produces growth, stagnation, death. But the pendulum of change seemed to swing out of sync from its expected course. Both Jack and Pete began introducing more complex sounds into the music, experimenting with new rhythms and instruments. Their production decreased as they spent time retooling the structure of their music. Because of her proximity to the group, Nikki didn't recognize her introduction into their mix as part of this process. She constituted yet another tree in their forest of change.

Grant didn't escape unscathed from this strange itchiness either. Taking Nikki's presence for granted once they became "legal," he left her in charge of their public persona to turn inside himself, spending hours alone with his new sitar creating his own sound, writing out his lyrics. He gave birth to disjointed, jangled sounds with nonsensical words. Nikki thought of them as themes in search of a topic. Seeking to understand what obviously meant so much to her husband, she engaged him about his themes. Icily, he met her queries with "If you don't get it, I won't waste my time explaining it to you." On his days off, he'd seal himself off for hours companioned only by a vacant stare and the strains of Middle Eastern music saturating the room. He excused his behavior as getting in tune with the new stop on the tour, India. Nikki didn't realize he had dived headlong into the world of "mind expansion" and dropping acid.

In her innocence, Nikki also failed to recognize the recent sweet smell of pot floating through the hotel rooms. Alcohol no longer stilled the restless beast. Narcotics became the logical next step to quell the anxiety from induced captivity. Hiding their use from her, the group retreated for vast periods and disguised its smell with incense. Compelled, Mary pulled her aside and enlightened her. Nikki felt violated. She didn't know whether they kept her on the outside for her protection or out of paranoia. But their banishment stung. Their drug use, compounded by their secrecy, chafed relations.

The group always enjoyed touring the Southern Hemisphere in January and February. The southern summertime weather offered a welcome respite from the frigid north. But more changes loomed on the horizon. On the permissive beaches of South America, the group caught glimpses of Jack with a naked, dark-haired beauty; her almost

Godiva-length hair barely covered her charms. Later, Solana clung on his arm through parties absent the press. Continually, she joined him as they crossed the southern continent. With her obvious presence, the group grew nervously restive. Nikki struggled between protecting Candy from the news and revealing it to her. Her kinship with Jack dissolved into a gnawing, internal loathing. And Grant dodged all her overtures on the subject.

Each day the intolerability built. Jack now brought Solana to every performance, every recording session. The mounting tension pressurized them. Nikki couldn't let her personal feelings toward Jack affect her performance onstage, so she focused on her fans. In so many ways, they became her saving grace.

After four weeks of her protracted "tolerance," Nikki resolved to tell Candy. She determined it had to be done in person, not over the phone. Since Solana's presence also angered Pete and Richie, she wanted their endorsement of her plan—but drew up short. Involving Pete and Richie constituted drawing a line in the sand and asking the four to choose up sides. Nikki knew if she forced them to choose, then *she'd* be responsible for the demise of the Merseymen, not Jack, not Solana. A bridge too far to cross.

Grant exploded with a round of viperous expletives when she told him of her plan to make Candy aware of Jack's infidelity. Unhinged, he cornered her several times in the too-small suite, threatening her with raised fists. In harassing, guttural tones, he verbally battered her. Grant accused her of trying to break up the group. His newfound aggressive hostility confounded her. Without laying a hand on her, Grant pummeled her.

Pulled apart on the inside, she fled their suite. Desperate, she walked out of the hotel, into the night, looking for answers. To Nikki, her silence—their silence—constituted tacit approval. How could she remain silent, but how should she speak up?

Operating on autopilot, as if invisible, Nikki ducked out of their hotel in Buenos Aires. She didn't even bother to look before entering the street to scout for fans, media, or the like. Her plan only included walking until she found her answers.

Preoccupied by her dilemma, she failed to notice the two dark figures approaching fast from behind. As they closed in, their scuffling, quickening footsteps and furtive whispers woke her to imminent danger, sadly too late for evasive action. Suddenly, viselike hands gripped both her arms, arresting Nikki in her tracks. Her captors read the fear in her startled eyes. Her fright enticed them; feeding their depraved hunger, they shoved her against a brick building. Its uneven surface dug into Nikki's back. Streetlights flashed across their swarthy faces, gnarled with several days' growth of beard. Lust from heathen red eyes leered at her. Their filthy fingers lifted bits of her clothing as they examined the merchandise. Hissing, they threw barbs and taunting jeers through their missing and jagged teeth. The exhaust of raw hooch reeked from their pores.

They infused her with their venom of panic. Nikki struggled, reflexively trying to kick her way free. Instantly, their legs spread and pinned hers, splaying her spread eagle against the wall. Desperately, she tried to wipe away her panic. They took turns grinding their mouths against her lips, tasting the promise of the sweet fruit of conquest. Their sandpaper stubble burned Nikki's lips and face. She pitched her head side to side to avoid contact. With a free hand, one captor grabbed a thatch of hair, yanking her head back with a sharp rap against the bricks. The other unleashed the back of his hand against her cheek. Nikki closed her eyes. The slap echoed in her ears, snapping her head from the other's hold, sending her cheekbone— *whack*—into the wall. The energy of the violence charged his spirit. He centered her head on the stone surface and swung again. *Smack!* Her lips parted, and she tasted the brick. Something warm ran into Nikki's mouth. His hand moved to the collar of her blouse. He loaded his fist with a hefty helping of material and ripped—exposing her.

Dazed, Nikki heard the urgent, swift footfalls of others approaching. Were these two merely advance men for a descending swarm? She heard the shattering of glass. Broken glass terrified her. Were the new recruits armed with those razor-sharp shards? Blindly, her mind raced to find escape before their reinforcements arrived.

In one fell movement, white flesh of forearms straddled her captors' throats; their eyes bulged out. Hands seized their wrists, wrenching them up along their backs. In pain, they writhed facedown to the ground, their arms thrust back, way above their heads. A boot to the ass sent them in a crawling slither along the sidewalk. They scuttled off into the blackness.

Unsupported, Nikki collapsed, shuddering to the ground. She tried to gather her legs under her for a retreat from the new vanquishers but couldn't locate any power. Strong hands under her arms lifted her up. Nikki sobbed at the inevitability of impending doom.

"Goodnight! It is her!" said one voice.

"Here, give her to me," another whispered. Nikki felt herself being laid onto someone's chest. His arms encompassed her; his hands smoothed her hair. He spoke in consoling tones. "It's okay. It's okay. You're with friends." He covered her with his jacket.

"Get a cab," the man quietly commanded. Fearing more faces of the beast, Nikki finally summoned the nerve to look at the person who held her. She looked up straight into Karl's face.

Gently, the reporter smiled at her. "It's okay. You're okay now." He continued to smooth her hair and dab at the warm fluid from near her eye. She clutched tighter into his chest, unable to say anything; an irrepressible whimper emanated from deep inside of her. Gradually shaking off the trauma, reality came in incoherent, halting waves. Nikki tried to sit on her own, but her strength didn't follow. A taxi screeched to a stop at the curb, and Karl's friend came around to help scoop her up into the waiting car.

Karl draped her arms around his neck. Nikki willed them to grab on, but they fell back limp on her. Her shoe dragged across some glass. It tinkled on the sidewalk as they loaded her into the taxi.

Karl spoke softly. "Nikki. I'm going to have the driver take us back to your hotel. Don't worry. I'll get you back to Grant."

Instantly, her eyes widened in dread. She thrashed back and forth. A rush of breath escaped from her swollen lips. "No. No!"

Karl calmed her. "Okay. Okay, we'll do something else. Shh, don't worry." He muttered as he thought, "Nikki, I'm going to take you to my hotel. Is that all right?" Quietly, she settled back into his arms.

Karl had the cabbie park in the hotel's underground garage. He sent his friend in to retrieve a hat, sunglasses, his topcoat, and a wheelchair from the hotel. He intended to pass Nikki off as an eccentric pal who consumed a little too much nightlife. Using the lengthy topcoat to obscure her form, Karl pulled the hat down to the bridge of the glasses to hide most of her contusions. As anticipated, the wheelchair raised red flags with the night manager. He insisted on sending up the hotel's doctor on call.

Karl laid Nikki on his bed, standing at her side during the doctor's examination. The doctor concluded that probably nothing was broken; however, she had likely suffered a concussion. With his penlight, he searched for signs of bleeding behind her eyes and warned of the dangers of swelling brain tissue. Adeptly, the physician butterflied pieces of tape and placed them above Nikki's left eye, to close the wound. Adamantly, he recommended the hospital for X-rays and extensive examination. He left prescribing ice for the swelling, aspirin for the pain, constant supervision for the concussion along with a list of warning signs, in case the concussion took a turn for the worse. The doctor never recognized the identity of his patient.

Drawing up a chair alongside the bed, Karl dialed the phone.

"Hello, Bruce? Karl Nielson here. There's been a bit of an accident... No. No, nothing serious, but I'd like you to come over to my hotel directly. I'm at the Hilton... No, it's best not to discuss it over the phone. I'll explain when I see you. Don't worry, just please hurry." He hung up.

In the meantime, Karl and his friend fluffed a considerable stack of pillows to prop Nikki up into a semisitting position. Knowing she had to remain conscious for twenty-four hours, he sent down for a carafe of strong coffee for his vigil and a pitcher of fruit juice for her. Nikki hardly possessed enough energy to draw the fluid up through the straw. When she did, the juice's mild acid stung her lips. In her detached state, she wondered about the red splotches on Karl's shirt. Gradually biting pain replaced the fuzziness. She couldn't control an internal trembling.

Panicked by Karl's call, Bruce grabbed Mary to go with him. Not knowing what to expect, on the ride over, Mary prepared herself for all the ghastly possibilities so she could stem any emotional outburst. But Bruce's horrified reaction as he stood in the doorway telegraphed to Nikki the grim reality of her condition.

"Cor, Karl! What happened?" Bruce gasped as he rushed in.

"A couple of street thugs jumped her."

"Where in the hell was Jarred from security?" demanded Bruce.

"I don't know. She probably ditched him. We were on our way to clear up some of the scheduling conflicts with Jarred, when we saw Nikki slip out of a side exit of the hotel. On a whim we followed her, just to see what she was up to. I guess we gave her too much lead. Within about ten blocks from the hotel, two thugs cut into her from an alleyway. My photographer Jimmy and I ran up the street as fast as possible, but unfortunately, they got their hooks into her before we could get there. This is how we found her. They roughed her up pretty good."

Remotely, Nikki heard all their words, but nothing registered.

Bruce turned to Nikki. "Nicole, are you all right? Do you need anything?"

Vacantly, she blinked at him.

Wrinkling his face in distress, he revolved back to Karl. "Why in the bloody hell didn't you bring her back to our hotel and Grant?"

At that, Nikki fussed profusely under the covers.

Karl sternly put his finger to his lips, directing the gesture toward Bruce. Soothingly, he patted Nikki's arm. "It's okay. You're fine here. Don't worry."

Then Karl directed his attention back to Bruce. "I don't understand it. Of course, that's the first place I tried to take her. But any mention of Grant and she reacts that way. She hasn't spoken except to say no when I asked her about going to him. It's almost like she connects him with the attack. Has something happened?"

"I dunno. But she's his wife. I can't hide this from him. He has to be told."

"Of course... The doctor examined her just before you came. He wanted to admit her to the hospital immediately, but that's your call. He said she probably suffered a concussion. Nothing appears broken."

While the two men discussed options, Mary administered sips of juice along with applying cold compresses. After listening to the men's fruitless conjecture, Mary offered an idea of her own. "How about if we tell Grant that the scuffle occurred near Karl's hotel? Because he was afraid to move her too much, he brought her to his suite. Other than going to the hospital that the doctors don't want her moved. So I am sitting up with her. Grant should buy that. If she's scared of Grant, you could send her into a delirium by introducing him now. We have to buy her some time until she's out of the woods and you have all the facts."

The two accepted her plan. As it turned out, Bruce couldn't find Grant anyway until the following midday when he showed up for the concert.

By midmorning, Nikki had recovered enough to take light toast and tea for breakfast. Mary helped her shower and gently washed and fixed her hair. Bruce sent over a change of clothes. Under her own power, Nikki faced the inevitable—her image in the mirror. White butterfly bandages closing the cut above her left eye stood in stark contrast to the swelling and the iridescent purple of the bruises. The right side of her lip ballooned to double its normal size. A bluish pallor clung to Nikki's cheeks. Assorted bruises, including her assailants' handprints on Nikki's wrists, peppered her entire body. The trembling remained.

Bruce canceled Nikki's afternoon concert appearance with the excuse of stomach flu.

Following the concert, Grant summoned an adequate amount of concern and rushed to Nikki's bedside. She stiffened when she woke, and his frame filled the doorway. Mary squeezed her hand in support. Sitting up tall in the chair beside the bed, with terrier zeal, Mary fiercely guarded her charge.

Grant approached slowly, gallantly, practically dropping to one knee, ignoring Nikki's protector. Gently taking her hand, he kissed it. "Oh, luv, are you all right? I came as soon as I could. How do you feel?" He lavished her fingertips with kisses.

"I'm getting better. Oh, Grant, it was so—"

Tenderly, he interrupted, "Mary, you can leave us now. I'll take it from here."

Coldly, she held her ground. "It's okay, Grant. I don't mind."

Resolutely, Grant insisted, "Mary, I'd like some time alone with my wife."

Nikki smiled limply, ceding Mary permission to depart. She blamed her apprehension of her husband on the concussion. Desperately, she needed her prince now to sweep her up in his arms and tenderly kiss away all the fears and the ugliness of the previous night. Grant ushered Mary out, closing the door on the heels of her exit.

Assuming his position at the foot of her bed, Grant snapped, "Well, ain't you a sight! Do we need to buy you an attack dog to take along now?"

Confused by the brusque change, Nikki weakly smiled at him. "I suppose so."

"So, Nik, how did this happen?" He abandoned all concern, scolding her like an errant child.

Taken aback, she mumbled, "These guys grabbed me."

"And what in the bleedin' hell were you doin' out walkin' after dark? Have all yer senses left ya?"

"I needed some time to think things through."

"Think? About what? Oh, so this is how you punish me for our li'l row!" Grant turned it all around, victimizing himself, erasing her attackers.

"You?"

"Yeah, me. Furthermore, you missed the concert this afternoon. Or do ya care? The career ya wanted so badly? Now ya can't bother to show up to play the gig! We had to cover for ya. And all the blokes askin' about ya! What did the Princess need—more attention?"

Nikki couldn't believe her ears. She felt disconnected, like she failed to track the conversation. "No, really, these guys jumped out—"

"Did you set this whole thing up so you could spend time with yer li'l reporter boyfriend? Gettin' 'im to feel sorry for ya. Grabbin' a li'l more free press! And who knows what else!" His acid words scalded her.

Advancing, Grant stripped the covers from her, grabbing for her arm.

Nikki cowered.

"Get up, bitch! Get yer hussy li'l ass together. Yer goin' home with me!" Grant clenched her right forearm. With his entire force, he yanked her up out of bed.

White-hot searing pain coursed through her shoulder. A cry of pain involuntarily escaped from the depth of her soul.

In a flash, Karl burst through the doors. Mary came on his heels.

Grant froze, his hand still wrenching Nikki's arm.

Nikki crumpled.

Grant dropped her arm.

Mary rushed to catch her.

Grant squared off with Karl.

Karl answered with a resounding blow to the jaw, sending Grant reeling backward, careening into a chair then to the floor.

Grant struggled to get his feet under him.

Karl grabbed the throat of his shirt, lifting him from the ground. He met Grant's face with a roundhouse punch, sending him sprawling to the floor. Karl lunged at Grant again, when Jimmy tackled him, grabbing his arms to break up the fight. Jimmy yelled Karl's name to jolt him back to reality. Finally, Karl shook himself free of the bloodlust and returned to rationality, sinking into a chair. Jimmy offered Grant a hand up.

Grant staggered to a sofa in the anteroom under his own power.

Wrapping some ice in a towel, Mary presented it to Grant for his eye. "Here! Use this. Grant, you need to get back to your hotel. I'll bring Nikki around in a bit. Now get." Opening the door, she prompted his exit.

Karl held his head, sitting in the chair. He knew he'd crossed the line. A reporter doesn't beat up the hottest tabloid property in the world. "Oh, I'm sorry, Nikki. I overheard. He made me crazy. I couldn't believe it. When you screamed, I just erupted. I'm sorry." He went over to the bed and picked up her hand. "But you know, I'd do it all again. I'm so glad we were around last night."

Nikki winced through the pain burning in her right shoulder. "I might not be alive today if it weren't for you. Karl, I can never thank you enough for saving me last night."

"I didn't rescue you last night so he could beat you up today. What's going on with you and Grant? Is he abusing you? Every time I mentioned his name last night, you cringed."

In denial, Nikki excused, "No! No, I'm not sure why. Maybe it's because we had an argument just before I left the hotel. Then the mugging, perhaps I associated Grant with the attack."

"Well, what in the hell got into him? His wife was just beaten, nearly raped, and killed; and he's making up stories of affairs and blaming you? Nikki, I just don't get it. But you know, I'll always be here for you—on or off the record. If you're up to it, we should get you back to your hotel now."

Mercifully, when they reached Nikki's hotel suite, Grant was nowhere to be found. Mary helped Nikki change, doled out more aspirin, and saw her back into bed.

Nikki woke sometime in the middle of the night to a man's hushed voice. The whisper called, "Nikki, are you asleep? Nikki. Nikki, wake up." Fighting to pull herself from sleep, she opened her eyes to see Grant sitting on the bed, his bloodshot brown eyes pleading her to consciousness.

"Wake up, Nikki. I need you. I've been such a bloody fool." Grant sputtered tears. "I nearly lost you. How could I have said those awful things? What would I do without you? They almost killed you." Gaining in emotional volume, his sobs racked his body. His movement on the bed refreshed the pain in her shoulder, but Nikki willed the pain into the background. Grant needed her.

Crawling in next to her, once again he reeked of gin and incense. "I can't lose you. I can't lose you," he repeated through gasps for breath. "I don't know what came over me. Maybe I just got scared. Can you forgive me? Please? Please forgive me."

She hushed him with comforting succor.

By morning, her shoulder raged with pain, stabbing her awake. Nikki got up before she disturbed Grant and shuffled into the living room of the suite. The pain twisted her into knots, driving her into a chair, making her sick to her stomach. To quiet the nausea, she pulled her legs up to her chest. She phoned Mary. Without asking permission, Mary brought Bruce and the hotel doctor.

Bruce never questioned Nikki's shoulder injury; he assumed it to be a latent consequence of the mugging. Everyone agreed Nikki needed to be seen immediately at the hospital. Bruce and Mary hastily assembled a cover story for her hospital visit.

All the commotion in the suite brought Grant out of the bedroom. His face, with a shiner below his left eye, begged the question.

"What the hell happened to you?" Bruce asked in shock.

In unison, the room's attention swung to Grant, waiting for his explanation. Karl, Nikki, and Mary knew his reply would set the parameters of Nikki's future business relationship with Karl. Did Grant hate Karl enough to cough up his vicious accusations from the night before, thereby forever poisoning the water between Karl and Nikki? Or did his manhandling of Nikki disturb him enough to lie?

Armed with the truth and not afraid to use it, Mary shot Grant an admonishing look, warning him not to interfere.

Carefully, Grant considered the double-edged possibilities of his answer. "I... I did a stupid thing. Last night I went looking for the bastards who knocked Nikki about. Of course I didn't find them, but I stumbled into a bar long enough to get into a row of my own." Guilt forced Grant's hand. He lied with stone-cold abandon!

Then he turned his attention to Nikki. "What do you think, luv? Shall we be photographed with our matching shiners? Bravely together even to the end!" Threateningly, he narrowed his eyes. In other words, he expected Nikki's silence in return for his lie.

Nikki didn't realize that in the bargain, her silence tacitly granted permission for further abuse. Involuntarily, a gasp escaped from Mary when Nikki demurred, "Sure."

Jarred, Nikki's head of security, assisted her to the limo. Mildly, he rebuked her, "Nikki, please, you really have to let me do my job. If you want to go out again, let me go with you or send someone.

Okay? I don't ever want to see something like this happen again to you. This really tears me up."

Nikki met his caring eyes. "I promise, Jarred. From now on, I'll let you know."

CHAPTER 11

★

Teetering

After the required X-rays, poking and probing, the hospital's medical team assessed Nikki's condition as a dislocated right shoulder and immediately sedated her to realign the joint. When Nikki emerged from the anesthesia, Grant recited the litany of dreadful news as the doctors had delivered it to him: twelve weeks of complete rest followed by four weeks of therapy. It meant canceling Nikki's part of the tour and sending her home. Uncharacteristically, Grant assumed the reins of authority. Tenaciously, he denied Nikki's pleas to stay, insisting she recuperate under her mother's care in Pennsylvania. Mary would accompany her. Grant ended the discussion by presenting her next dosage of painkillers, which returned her to unconsciousness.

A sense of finality—an end to her days with the Merseymen—brushed across Nikki's mind, insinuating itself into her departure. In a stupor of prescribed medications, Nikki didn't remember anything about the flight. Mary helped her stumble through customs and into her parents' welcoming arms before Mary changed planes to go to her home in Virginia.

For the next two days, dreams of evil, twisted, taunting faces with searing red eyes tortured Nikki's sleep. Having enough of their daughter's drug-induced coma, Fran called their family physician to see if he concurred with doctors in Argentina.

"Heavens, Frances, why would they keep her in a coma? If the shoulder is aligned properly, the pain should be gone. Stop the pain pills! And bring her in when she's conscious," Dr. Hess ordered.

After his examination, Dr. Hess shook his head in disbelief. "I don't understand. The shoulder's been correctly placed. Why prescribe immobilization for twelve weeks? In addition, there's no sign of any lingering effects from the head trauma. Why dope her up like this? Maybe I'm missing something that doctor saw in his examination. Could you get me his name, Nicole? I'd like to get in touch with him."

Her mother assured her Grant had called each evening since she arrived home. Nikki waited for Grant's nightly call so she could get the information for Dr. Hess.

Over the dinner table that evening, her mom couldn't restrain herself anymore, "Nikki, what happened to you in Buenos Aires?"

Nikki furnished all the details of the attack and Karl's lifesaving rescue but omitted Grant's violent mood swing.

"So your shoulder was dislocated during the attack?" her dad questioned.

"I suppose so," Nikki fudged, not wishing to cast Grant in the light he deserved.

"I don't understand how the doctor could have missed that on the first go-round. It must have hurt you terribly?" Richard fished on.

"I had so much pain, I guess I couldn't tell one from the other." *There, did he buy that?*

The phone interrupted their dance. Fran answered Grant's call, checking in.

Taking the phone from her mother, in the background, Nikki heard the strains of Middle Eastern music. "Hi, Grant. I miss you. What's going on?"

"So you're up. The doctor wanted you medicated for at least a week. And what do you mean seeing another doctor? What's the matter? Don't you trust me?"

"What's trust got to do with it? Mom and Dad weren't too sure about the doctors down there. Dr. Hess is confused by their diagnosis. He needs to talk to the doctor from the hospital. Do you have his name?"

"I dunno. Maybe Bruce has it. Well, gotta go."

"Wait, Grant. I need—"

The connection went dead. Grant never called again.

The next day, Nikki tried Bruce, but the harried manager didn't have the details from the doctor. Instead, he carped about deteriorating conditions of the tour before cutting Nikki short.

Tears pooled in Nikki's eyes as she turned to her parents. "I don't understand. What's happening? No one can talk."

"Try Mary down in Virginia. Maybe she's heard something," Richard suggested.

Fortuitously, a call from Mary interrupted them. "Nikki? You're not going to believe this! Ben called today. Seems everything has fallen apart on the tour. Rumors about you are rampant. They say you're near death, you're paralyzed, even insane and committed to an asylum. It's causing hysteria. Every day the headlines get worse. And it's spreading to Europe. Grant has told them you're in a coma, and your parents are near mental collapse. Bruce can't control what's going on."

"Mary, I don't understand Grant's lies. None of that rubbish is true. My parents are here with me. We've got to put an end to the rumors. Where's Karl? Can he help?"

"Ben told me that Grant banished Karl yesterday. He accused him of arranging your mugging just to sell papers. He's threatened to file assault charges and a lawsuit, claiming Karl's presence compromises his ability to perform. He demanded Karl's touring pass."

"Mary, that's all a lie! Can't someone say anything?"

"Go against Grant Henderson? Not likely, especially since he's your husband."

"Can you catch a flight up here to Pennsylvania, Mary? We need to talk!"

"Sure. I'll be there tomorrow morning. Besides, there's something else we have to discuss." She hated to leave Nikki hanging, but she wasn't about to lay her next bit of news on Nikki over the phone. Saturated already by Grant's antics, Nikki didn't press her further.

Before ringing off, Nikki asked Mary to get the attending physician's report from the Buenos Aires hospital.

Unsuccessfully, Nikki tried to reach Karl at his London flat so the three of them could work on a plan.

At nine that night, headlights crawled down the driveway. Richard admitted the caller. "Look, Nikki, Karl stopped by on his way back to London," her father called up the stairs to her.

Her parents stayed only long enough to express their gratitude for his heroics, then suggested she and Karl might talk in comfort in the study.

Exhausted, Karl peeled off his winter topcoat, draping it over one of the leather wingback chairs. Nikki invited him to sit. Overriding concern muted her delight at seeing her friend. "Karl, what's going on? Mary said Grant expelled you."

"My questions first. What about you? I called your parents a couple of days after you left to check on you. They told me about your doctor's assessment. That didn't square with all the press's hand-wringing. Ace reporter that I am, I went directly to Grant and questioned him. He had me thrown out on my ear. The bugger seems to be hatching some sort of scheme. Do you know what he's after?"

"No. But evidently it includes cutting me out of the picture. He's upset that I'm conscious and ambulatory. Then he hung up on me and won't take any of my calls."

For the next three hours, Karl and Nikki tried to piece together the puzzle of Grant's offbeat, uncharacteristic movements. Nikki even confessed Grant's flip-flop on her career, his drug use, his mood swings, and his mysterious disappearances. The lateness of the hour finally shut them down, and Nikki invited Karl to stay in the guest bedroom.

Mary arrived the following day bringing the remaining two puzzle pieces. She had spoken to the attending emergency room physician. Recalling the case vividly, he remembered he had recommended two weeks in the sling, without calling for bed rest. He only prescribed the narcotics under duress. Grant had begged for them fearing Nikki's pain might become debilitating, and then being hundreds of miles away, they wouldn't be able to get the medication. Under Grant's resolute persistence, the doctor acquiesced.

Mary swallowed hard to bolster her determination before delivering the last resounding bit of information. "Jack isn't the only one with a bird on the side. Grant has been keeping company outside your bed too."

Genuinely overcome, Nikki sank back into her chair. "Are you sure?"

"Yes. God have mercy, yes. In fact, that's why Bruce couldn't find Grant the night of the mugging."

"Who, Mary? Who is it?" Nikki wanted to know.

"Evidently, there have been many, but recurrently it's been a model from their first movie, Bridget. This isn't idle speculation. Ben told me the other night. He found out when he and Richie got 'in their cups.' Since Richie's marriage, Grant's behavior really bothers him. With courage from a bottle of scotch, he confessed all the sordid details to Ben." Mary paused. "Nikki, I'm so sorry."

"No, it's okay. This clears up a whole lot. Is Grant planning on a divorce?"

"I don't know. Ben says he still pretends to be devastated by your absence."

"How long has it been going on?"

"Evidently since their first movie."

The longevity of his infidelity left Nikki reeling. "Does everyone know?"

"Probably. Bridget does drugs with Grant. He's planning on taking her on the tour to India, since you won't be along."

At that point, Nikki's parents wandered into the kitchen, and Nikki invited them into the conversation. In utter honesty, she broke the entire story to them, including Grant's violence.

In Nikki's recounting for her parents, a light dawned on Karl. "No wonder he cooked up that cock-and-bull story about me before he sacked me! I had enough information to be considered dangerous, and with my investigative background, I might have stumbled onto the rest of this entire bloody mess."

"Then his guilt drove him to fire you?" Nikki interrupted.

"Maybe," Karl tossed back.

"Or the acid? Or…" Nik continued to sort out excuses.

Impatiently, her father jumped in, "Or a thousand things! Maybe *you'll* never know. That's spilled milk. Right now you have to ask yourself some tough questions."

"Like?" Nikki led, although her heart already knew those questions.

"Can you trust him? Will you stay with him? Where does this leave your career? You get my drift, and you can probably come up with a few questions yourself." Frustrated, unable to take the retaliatory action his paternal instinct demanded, the entire recital boiled beneath her father's skin. Aggravated, Richard exited the room.

Karl understood the potent masculine emotional quagmire arresting Richard. He recognized it from his own primal male response in the hotel that night. Likewise, he joined Richard outside for a breath of air.

Meanwhile, Nikki struggled with the implications of the assembled puzzle. Thoughts and flashbacks vacillating between the past to the present overwhelmed her. She recalled the nights early in their marriage—his late comings from costume fittings, the gin on his breath. Was that one of his trysts? Skipping ahead, the pictures of all the dollies on his arm. Was it really just for publicity? Back to the fight in his dressing room when Nikki condemned him to a night on his couch. Did Bridget share it too? Fast forward again to last summer and the tabloid accounts of affairs with hot models during their separate summer tours. Was that the American press run amok or reality? The night of Nikki's attack, was Grant wrestling Bridget under the covers in the hours when he couldn't be found? "What a fool I've been!" Nikki lamented, tasting self-pity. "What did I do to cause him to do this?"

"Nothing," Fran answered frostily, annoyed by a situation over which she had no control and compounded by her daughter's turn to self-sympathy.

"Could it have been my career? Was it the separation? Was it the road?"

"Stop it, Nicole!" Fran's sharp tone demanded Nikki's attention. "Yes, all those things might have strained your relationship. A mature person talks about the pressures and finds solutions. You grow together that way. Everything you mentioned might have fueled Grant's alienation, but he should have talked to you. Nothing justifies his actions. And *nothing* warrants his abuse of you."

Drawing herself alongside Nikki's chair, she cast a judicious eye at her. "So, Nicole, how long are you going to wallow in self-pity?" More between-the-eyes parenting. "What are *you* going to *do* about this?"

Nikki rose to meet her mother's tough love standards. "I guess I had better talk to Grant about us. I have to find out what drove him to do this and what we can do to fix it. But I won't compromise my principles. I won't share him. I won't do drugs."

Her mom patted her hand. "There you go. That's the woman I raised. That's all you can do, Nikki. And then be prepared to back up his answers with your own course of action."

To clear her head and get a fresh perspective, that afternoon Nikki rode Thunder down the dirt road to her old haunt at the lake. The weather had brightened that first of February, melting all the snow, leaving in its wake the musty sweet smell of moist, promising earth. Approaching in the distance, coming around a curve in the road, another horse and rider caught Nikki's attention.

The horse, of jumping stock, stood tall, with exquisitely etched features born of well-chosen bloodlines. His finely maintained coat radiated in the sun. The nobility of the steed perfectly matched his rider, who sported tall riding boots, jodhpurs, suede blazer, and an ascot. The sun warmed the gold of his sandy-blond hair. Perfectly seated, he cantered toward Nikki. An unusual pair, their stylish presentation reaped her fascination. Nikki prepared a customary greeting as their paths bypassed.

However, in the final seconds, horse and rider moved to intersect her path, pulling up to face Nikki and Thunder. Instantly, she recognized the rider as the mysterious man from Naples. He nodded his head in a greeting. "Good morning. It's certainly good to see you recovering and on your feet again. I hope you are feeling well?"

"Yes, I am. Thank you for asking." The knowledge of her convalescence and his presence muted her response.

"You have my fervent prayers for a complete recovery. It warms my soul to see you looking so fit. No wonder the sun is smiling today. It's trying to match your radiance. *Vaya con Dios*." He clucked to his horse. In a striking manner, the steed reared up, and the pair left in a dashing gallop. Thunder swung around so they could watch them disappear down the road.

The stranger's appearance on the road both enchanted and unnerved Nikki. *Is he following me? How is it he keeps turning up— and now at my parents' home? Who exactly is he? He always has the most charming air to him, but is he stalking me?* He ruined her contemplative morning at the lake. The more Nikki tried to concentrate on the matter at hand with Grant, the more the stranger's image, rising up on the road, captured her imagination.

Back at the house, Karl, Mary, and Nikki again gathered around the table to come up with a plan for combating the awful rumors about Nikki. Mary detailed the Merseymen's latest itinerary. "They'll leave South America in three days. Rather than head off directly to India, the entourage will go back to London for a week before their two-week run at India and Pakistan."

"We have to get the good news out about Nikki's condition," Karl added. "Let's hire a camera crew from here to film Nikki's recovery story and apology for worrying her fans. I'll do the interview."

"And I can have it on the air in two days in Nikki's markets. The gossip circuit will suck up the piece immediately," Mary countered. "Then the news outlets will incorporate it into their information stream."

Following the taped interview later that afternoon, the three left for London. While Karl and Mary attended to the piece's final details, Nikki would have her little tête-à-tête with Grant.

Lying low at Mary's London flat, Nikki prepared for Grant's return from South America. She grew nervous over her impending showdown. How she despised confrontation; she wished she could put it off forever. Yet she wanted to confront him *now*, to get the matter over with.

Nikki knew her early return from her convalescence would shock everyone. Since Grant hadn't been congenial on the phone, Nikki wondered how the rest of the guys felt about her now. Not wanting to meet him alone, Nikki decided it would be best to expose her presence to Grant in public at the recording studio. That plan would afford Grant time to mask his probable apoplectic outrage at her presence. Hopefully, the others would surround her with their support for her early return. Given time, Grant may even compose himself enough to feign a tender hug and kiss. With the tension diffused, later Nikki and Grant could have a nonconfrontational discussion. Her entire plan would be out the window, however, if Grant had contaminated the group to her return and they greeted her with embarrassed silence. Then divvying up the spoils of a career and a ruined marriage would be her legacy. Dismissing such thoughts as negative energy, she refused them power.

Nikki assembled her costume for the encounter—an essay of health and desire. She chose a deep-cut, V-neck, formfitting red bodysuit with a black leather micromini and red sheer stockings to display her lengthy legs. Seductively, she unleashed her hair.

At two, Nikki waltzed into the control booth to the delighted amazement of Bruce and Ben. Abandoning their positions at the controls, they grabbed her up in their enthusiasm and burst through the door into the studio itself.

"Hey, lads!" Bruce crowed. "Look who's here!"

Beaming, Nikki threw open her arms in a "ta-da" pose. Instinctively, her eyes searched out Grant. As expected, staggering shock engulfed him. Quickly, she redirected her gaze and ceded him the privacy to collect himself.

The Merseymen surrounded her with their welcoming acclamation until Nikki became lost in their hugs and kisses. Finally, one elated reveler spun her around and encompassed her in his arms.

"Oh, luv! I can't believe ye'r home!" She found her lips locked to Grant's, who seemed earnestly euphoric at her homecoming. Nikki's heart wondered if their encounter would be easier than she had expected. Her father's phrase "trust, but verify" flashed to mind. Nikki vowed she wouldn't be swept up in the moment and dissuaded from her mission. Grant glued Nikki to his side as the recording session wrapped for the day in a delirious celebratory conclusion.

They partied like the "good old days" rocking on until the guys packed Grant and Nikki into a limo with lusty slaps on the back and knowing winks. Seizing the moment, Grant ran his fingers down Nikki's long stockinged legs, then up, up underneath her skirt, his mouth kissing hers deeply. Nikki matched his passion, tearing off his turtleneck.

Wickedly, Grant growled into her ear, "Cor! How I want you. But I'll take you at home. I want you in *our* bed."

Nikki grabbed him *there*, purring, "I can hold on as long as you. And I promise, you won't be disappointed."

Nikki ran ahead of Grant into the house, laughing, teasing him. Grabbing a bottle of champagne, she bolted up the stairs to their bedroom. She sat on the bed with the bottle wedged between her thighs; Grant swaggered in, leaned against the jamb, and watched. Slowly, she worked the cork back and forth, easing it out with her thumb and forefinger, releasing it with a plump pop. Holding his eyes in a kittenish tease, Nikki swigged from the bottle; she never released Grant's eyes. Rushing to the bed, he grabbed the bottle. Covering the hole with his thumb, he shook it vigorously. The effervescent liquid erupted, drenching Nikki in its spray. Giggling, she dared him—taunted him. With reckless abandon, he fulfilled his wish and reclaimed his wife in their marital bed.

Before closing her eyes in sleep, a thought crept in and gnawed at Nikki. *Was that fabulous lovemaking session just Grant's way of using me to erase her memory?* Nikki pushed the thought aside—morning would be soon enough to sort it all out.

With mixed feelings, Nikki rose to meet the morning, long before Grant stirred. Sitting with a steaming cup of tea, her knees drawn to her chest, Nikki watched the morning drizzle spot and trickle down the glass of the French doors. *I know last night's passion was a mistake. But maybe by giving in to the savage beast, I might win his confidence, break down his walls, and we can establish a lasting relationship.* Because she didn't want their important discussion derailed like last night, Nikki dressed conservatively that morning in jeans and a turtleneck.

Finally, Grant's slippered feet shuffled across the green slate of the kitchen floor. He enclosed her in his arms from behind. "Mmm… mornin', luv," he purred in her ear, nuzzling a kiss on her neck.

Rising to meet him, Nikki returned his embrace. "Good morning, my love." She kissed him then slipped out of his arms to get him his morning cup of tea.

Nerves dried out Nikki's throat—with a dryness no amount of tea could wash away. Her words stuck in her throat, but she summoned the courage. "Grant, we need to clear up some things. We need to talk."

"About what, luv?" He blithely maintained the charade.

"Dr. Hess called the physician in Buenos Aires. He said he never prescribed bed rest. And the drugs he prescribed were at your insistence. Did you lie to me? Were you trying to get rid of me?"

Grant hedged, "No. I was only thinking of you. I didn't want you to have any pain. I truly wanted you to get all the rest you needed so you could get better and we could enjoy our time together."

His explanation sounds so plausible. Have I blown this whole thing up out of context? Oh, how I want to lose myself in his explanation, to wrap myself in his arms and buy the fairy tale again! I could easily let everything else go, but Grant needs to answer one more question. Nikki swallowed. "What about Bridget?"

Grant's eyes widened at her knowledge. He leveled his gaze to meet hers. Caught, which way would he go? Nikki braced herself for his inevitable eruption of anger. Instead, puddles of tears formed in his soft brown eyes and leaked down his face. Gathering up her hands, he pressed them to his lips. His tears slid down Nikki's fingers. "How could I have been so stupid? She means nothing to me. You're everything I ever wanted. I missed you so much when you weren't by my side. I guess, I just got lost. I don't know what happened."

His tears cut inlets into her heart. But she went for broke anyway. "And the drugs? What about the drugs?"

Grant drew her in with his eye contact. The film of tears magnified the size of his eyes, turning them into heart-melting large watery pools. "You know she gave them to me. They made me crazy. I was high that night I hurt you. I didn't mean to. That's why I sent you away. I wanted to get straight for you. I couldn't hurt you again. I need you too much." Dropping off his chair, he fell to his knees, weeping into Nikki's lap. "I love you. I love you," he mumbled through his sobbing. "Please forgive me! Please!"

Nikki crumbled. Drawing him to her, she sealed the apology on his lips with a kiss. "Yes, Grant. I forgive you." Her eyes met his. "But this can never happen again. I can't do this again. Do you understand?" And her tears mingled with his in a compact of renewed love.

The rest of the day they refused to let go of each other. Grant canceled his appearance at the recording session. Nikki postponed her luncheon with Karl and Mary until the following afternoon. Instead, they drove to Cartier of London. Grant bought Nikki a symbol of their renewed love—entwined hearts of diamonds. Ordering a gourmet catered supper, they dined at home in front of their own blazing fireplace. A light snow fell outside. Bundling up, they walked the grounds of their estate in snow's frozen peace. On a stone bench by the cold black water stream, Nikki broached one more subject with Grant—that of Jack and Candy.

Grant's answer amazed Nikki. "Talk to Candy. I'm sure she knows by now, but she could probably use some comforting. The two of you can commiserate over the unfaithful louts you married."

Nikki blanched at Grant's all-too-real reference to himself.

"It's true, you know. Face the fact, I broke our vows. But it will never happen again. On my soul I promise."

The next afternoon, Grant drove Nikki to her favorite bistro (expensive enough to keep the groupies out) for lunch with Karl and Mary. He stunned everyone when he accompanied her to the table. Karl rose with uneasiness to meet Grant's extended hand.

Grasping Karl's hand, Grant spoke first. "What an appalling lout I've been. First, thank you for saving the life of my dear, sweet

Nikki. Second, I apologize for my bloody awful behavior. You were completely justified in belting me when I was crackers. Of course, you'll continue on with Nikki's publicity. Can't we just forget about this whole nasty episode?" He clasped Karl about the shoulders.

Astonished, Karl sputtered his acceptance.

"Well, I really must be running... Mary dear, good to see you." Turning, Grant passionately kissed Nikki goodbye. "See you at home, my love. Have a great afternoon." Then out he strode, the conquering hero.

Karl waited until Grant cleared the doorway. "Would someone mind telling me who in the hell was that? Nikki, what happened yesterday?"

Karl and Mary greeted Nikki's tale of the reformed Grant with guarded capitulation, urging caution.

Following lunch, Mary dropped Nikki at Candy's house. Candy met her with reddened eyes and a tear-swollen face. She already knew about Jack's unfaithfulness. Throwing her arms around her, Nikki entered. Candy's mother was keeping Jack Junior for a few days. The good friends cried together as Nikki recounted the entire saga about her decision to tell Candy about Jack and Solana, including the part about Grant's behavior and how they had just put their marriage back on track.

Candy hugged Nikki. "I know that you think the same thing can happen for us too. But it's too late." Candy's lip quivered. "Jack has asked me..." She took a deep breath to forestall another round of tears. "He wants to move Solana in with us! He wants a *ménage à trois*! But that's not all. He's brought home pot and acid. He says if I do these with them, it will open my eyes. I'll see he's right. I tried the pot. I won't do acid. Who'd take care of Jack Junior?" Candy erupted in a full-fledged wail.

"Oh, Candy, I couldn't stay under those conditions. I'd have to leave," Nikki consoled.

"That's what I want to do. But where will I go?"

"Go back to your parents' house. Get your own house. Better still, pack Jack's bags and toss the lout out. A proper attorney would tell you to do that."

Candy weighed the options as they discussed the consequences. Before Nikki left, Candy placed a phone call to a reputable attorney just for advice.

Grant understood. "What else can she do?" he lamented. "Jack brags about Solana and the drugs. Jack would like to see me so enlightened."

Nikki's blood boiled at the hint of Jack soliciting Grant's collusion. "Of course he would. It spreads the guilt. Then he's not the only lunatic. Grant, I can't pretend any longer everything's all right. You know how I feel about Solana and the drugs. I can't face Jack. I can't tell Candy to leave him and then stick around him because I'm making money with the group. That's two-faced. What if I bow out of the group?"

Grant concurred, "You have to do what you have to do. But understand I don't have that luxury. I have a commitment I must fulfill, no matter my personal feelings."

"I know," Nikki said as she cuddled into Grant's arms. "I won't leave your side though. I'll still travel with you. Just limit my exposure to Jack."

Grant enfolded her. "That's good because I want you with me." He kissed her. "You know you could still continue on your own from the recording studio."

"Anything, as long as we can be together. Then you agree about my leaving the group?"

Grant nodded. "I think it's best, although you may be committed for the India and Pakistan tour."

"I know. I'll talk to Bruce in the morning."

In Nikki's meeting with Bruce, he confirmed her obligation to perform in India and Pakistan. But more than anything, their discussion conflicted him. From the beginning, he had wanted to separate the two careers, but the combination act now drew a bigger gate than the Merseymen solo (a fact he completely kept to himself). Dare he tinker with that? And Bruce desperately wanted to avoid a confrontation with Jack at all costs. "Do us all a favor. Don't use the Solana thing as your reason for leaving. And please don't go toe to toe with

Jack. If you take a stand against him, he'll bloody well turn it into a war! Damn, he'd leave bodies all over the landscape!"

The tour of India and Pakistan devolved into a full-blown disaster for Nikki. By the second day, she came down with a torturous case of stomach flu, replete with nausea and vomiting. With heroic effort, Nikki held herself together for the concerts and press conferences. Likewise, Richie suffered a severe reaction to the spicy Indian food.

The rest of the group, however, developed an affinity for the Eastern culture and its sounds. Pete and Jack incorporated the Indian rhythms and musical phrasing into their work. Grant especially dove into every nuance of the Near Eastern culture. While Nikki hung over the toilet in between shows, he explored all the facets of Indian dynamism, occupying his time with side trips from the cities into the countryside. After a week and a half, when they reached Bombay, both Grant and Bruce insisted Nikki visit the British hospital there.

Following one of his little forays into the Indian civilization, Grant returned quite late to their hotel room. Nikki waited up for him with the physician's results.

CHAPTER 12

★

Falling

Nikki was almost three months pregnant. Her news caught Grant off guard. Since their reconciliation, she had grown accustomed to the caring side of Grant. Reveling in the news, Nikki embraced the incarnation of their love. Now she wanted Grant to share her joy—no matter how unexpected—a baby!

Mustering courage from his second gin and tonic, a hint of a smile pursed his lips. "Well then, we'll have a baby. I guess Richie and Doreen's baby will be only three months older than ours," Grant mused.

Five days later, following their last concert in Pakistan, Grant sent Nikki home to Pennsylvania to deliver the news to her parents in person. He wanted to stay on with Pete and Jack to do more exploring in his newfound promised land of India. He vowed to return to their Surrey home by March 1, 1966. Then they'd fill the nursery full of soft and cuddly baby things and await their new arrival.

Nikki's pregnancy gave Bruce the perfect alibi to retire Nikki from the combination act.

Richard and Fran's suspicions about the viability of Nikki's marriage, at first, muted their response to her news about the baby. But the inevitability of the event and the intriguing prospect of being grandparents won them over. Within days, Fran dragged Nikki through shopping malls in a buying spree of infant outfits in noncommittal yellows and greens.

The days flew by. Before Nikki knew it, her March 1 departure date was two days away, when Grant called. With sitar music echoing in the background, he explained how he had gotten a lot of good material, and he wanted to stay another week. They agreed to meet back in the Surrey house then.

But rather than rebook her flight to London, Nikki decided to catch her scheduled flight and get the house opened up properly to meet her arriving husband. At this point, Nikki's gushing maternal hormones drove a desire to feather her nest.

Despite the security, the large empty house scared Nikki at night, so Mary suggested Nikki bunk at her flat. By now her nausea had faded, but she couldn't shake being tired. The second day, they went over to the house and left the packages her mom bought for the baby, then hit the stores in another baby-shopping frenzy.

To announce the baby's arrival, work on her retirement from the combination act, and launch her solo career, Nikki scheduled a working lunch at Mary's flat. Karl joined them at ten; by eleven, Ben dropped by and stayed to participate.

They decided to minimize her departure from the guys by playing up the positive angles of a solo career. The baby, however, presented a whole other set of questions—When should she return to performing? Would she keep a rather low profile or tour again? And what about the American music scene? They thrashed out all those questions, and more, until three in the afternoon.

Karl ended their work session bemoaning the fact he hadn't had a tour of Nikki's house. "Here it is, March, and I haven't been asked to see it yet! I guess you have to be someone *really* special to be invited."

Immediately, Ben and Mary jumped on the bandwagon; and quicker than lickety-split, the four of them sardined themselves into Karl's mini Aston, heading out to Surrey.

Wanting to welcome her friends from inside so the fullness of the house's grandeur could fall on them, Nikki left her three friends standing on the front entry stoop while she ran around to the kitchen side door. On her hasty dash through the kitchen to the foyer, she noticed an empty gin bottle on the kitchen counter. *The maid must have forgotten to pitch that out in the rubbish,* she assessed.

With lavish flourish, Nikki swung the massive door open. "Please come in," she bade them enter, curtsying deeply. The stunning entry with its magnificent mahogany staircase, elegantly turned newels, and raised panels elicited gasps of awe from them. Both Ben and Karl rotated in place, drinking in the bravura of the entire foyer.

Suddenly, from the second floor, giggles floated down to them. Expecting the house to be empty, everyone exchanged inquiring glances. "The maid must be all atwitter over something," Nikki excused, as she started up the staircase to investigate.

More laughter met Nikki on the stairs. Leaping ahead, her mind attempted to prepare her for a variety of deeds that might be engaging the maid. *This all could be completely innocent, then we'll all have a good chuckle about it.* However, Nikki expected to find the worst. She wondered, *Never having fired anyone before, would a romp while on duty constitute grounds for the maid's dismissal?* At the landing of the second floor, she paused to determine the exact direction of the noise.

This time Nikki heard male undertones prompting what seemed to be sexually charged tittering, and they came from her bedroom! Once up the stairs, she listened at the door to solidify her suspicions before catching them in the act. More laughter. Incensed, *Son of a bitch! In my bed! On my time! Dismissal is the exact remedy!* Listening again, Nikki heard the high-pitched laughter of the coy feminine voice and a man teasing her.

It's Grant's voice! Quickly Nikki reassessed the circumstances. *Was that Grant entertaining in our bed? He wouldn't do that! He promised!* Not wanting to burst in with guns blazing to be wrong about it, Nikki listened again. Without question, the cooing and accompanying lusty chortles smacked of sexual foreplay. Nikki recognized Grant's line of patter. *Wow! How should I handle this? I'll meet the situation squarely, head-on, that's how.* Shelving the instinctive, injured ego reaction of screaming and raving, she replaced it with a cool, controlled air of authority. Snapping the handle, Nikki boldly pushed the door open.

There she sat naked, astraddle Grant. Her long strawberry-blond hair swung around through the air as she spun her head toward the noise of Nikki barging in the door. Her pert nipples stood erect on the firm breasts of her model-perfect, nubile body. Nikki recognized Bridget. Surprisingly, no one moved or dove for covers. The sweet odor of pot pervaded the room.

From flat on his back, Grant spouted protests.

Without spending time focusing on them, instead raising a convincing smile on her face, Nikki marched to the closet and returned with jeans and a pullover for Grant.

"Here, luv, put these on," she said in an everyday tone as if laying out clothes for a morning walk, then dropped his clothes in an unaffected manner next to him on the bed. "I'm afraid your afternoon festivities have come to an end. Your little friend will have to run on now. We are going to have some fun of our own."

Wrapping the sheet about her, Bridget ungracefully dismounted.

Determined to make the two of them wallow in their discomfort, Nikki refused them quarter. Instead, she leaned against the dresser, challenging Grant.

Red-faced, he angrily grabbed his pants and pulled them on his naked body, then his sweater. His nostrils flared under the heat of his embarrassment and growing temper. Rising up, he approached Nikki.

Standing her ground, erect, away from the dresser, they faced off, forgetting about the wench in the bed.

Grant beat Nikki to the first word, pushing his fingers into her chest. "What in the bleedin' hell are you doing here?" His eyes were on fire—his breath saturated with gin.

Nikki stepped back. "I came home to get things ready for you!"

"I didn't ask you to, now, did I?"

"I thought it would be the 'good wife' kind of thing to do. Obviously you don't want a good wife!" she spit.

"Well, Princess, as you can see, you should stick to the schedule. See, you get yourself in trouble when…you…don't…stick…to…the…schedule." His fingers poked her after each word, driving home the point.

Nikki backed up each time with his jabs.

Pulling herself up to make a stand, her eyes narrowed. "Grant, you promised your affair with her was over."

"Maybe it was. Maybe I could handle having you tied around my neck until you came up bleedin' pregnant!" No need for him to push that time. His words rocked her back on her heels.

Wrapped in the sheet, Bridget watched, blinking her vacuous green eyes.

Nikki used the jamb of the doorway to steady herself and come back at him. "So I was the millstone around your neck! Then why your tears? Why the apology? Why not just leave?"

Grant sneered contemptuously. "Just look around you, Nikki. Take a good, long, last look. You don't think I'd sacrifice all this for you, do you?" This time he shoved her with both hands into the hallway.

Anger and hostility swelled in her. "How long has it been going on this time?"

Grant laughed arrogantly. "This time? Why not just ask if it ever stopped! I just needed time." He jabbed her again. "Time to get all my things together."

"Oh! So you're leaving!"

He roared, "Leaving? I don't think so. You haven't been listening, Nikki dear." Bitterly, he derided her name, like a weapon against her, aggressively backing her farther and farther down the hall. "I'm getting things in order to get rid of *you*. The baby just delayed things a little, made the situation stickier. You're the one who's going. You didn't think for a moment that you'd get my career, my money, my house. No bleedin' way! I'm going to leave you like I found you, a poor twit from the country." He backed Nikki to within a few feet of the top of the stairs.

Enraged, rising up on her haunches, she fought back. "You can keep your precious money. And trust me I don't need *your* career. I've got one of my own that's going rather nicely. But, Grant, I *will* keep the house to raise our child in. He at least deserves that out of the drunken bastard he has for a father. So if you'll excuse me... I'm going to pack your things. Your little trollop can help you carry them

124

on your way out!" With a mighty shove, Nikki walked past him on her way to the bedroom.

Halfway down the hall, Grant chased Nikki until he latched on to her wrist, pulling her back to him. With a twisting wrench, he spun her around. Hate sparked in his eyes. "Come back here, you li'l bitch! Ye'r not going anywhere. I'm not through with you yet." He landed a wallop with the back of his hand against her face.

Momentarily, she fell back in shock. Grant read her body language as she reflexively shrank. Then he raised his hand to land another blow.

Something visceral from deep within Nikki cried out, *Enough!* Pulling up from her cower, she met his swing, blocking it with her forearm. Their arms clashed like swords in a duel. Steely-eyed, she defied him across their clenched stance. "So, Grant…hitting me makes you a big man? Then go ahead hit me again. Here, you haven't smacked me on this cheek." Boldly, she turned the opposite cheek toward him. "Hit me here. Go ahead, big man! Come on!"

Nikki's newfound aggression baffled him.

He dropped his cocked arm as she backed him down the hall. "What's the matter, Grant, no guts to beat up a woman? Come on, big man! Come on." She bullied him further, then pushed past him again on her way to pack his belongings.

Nikki almost made it to their bedroom door before he recovered from his amazement. He leaped at her—an uncontrollable juggernaut. From deep within him, a guttural growl grew. "Oh no, you don't! Come back here, you bloody bitch!"

His iron paws clamped onto her shoulders, heaving her into the hallway wall. Before Nikki could recover, he threw her into the opposite wall. She caromed off one wall to another, down the hall reeling, fighting to regain her balance before he threw her again. Nikki hit the banister railing. It stood her upright. She pushed off to bounce back and take another run at him.

Grant met her at the landing. Cocking his arm back, he loaded it up for another swing. He launched it. It came at her in slow motion. Desperately, frantically, Nikki searched for a way to escape the resounding blow. Even Grant's words reached her ears in the deep, halting baritone of slow motion. "Here…bitch…take…this."

The closed-fist blow connected with Nikki's right temple, propelling her off the top step, catapulting her in a lateral free fall. Instinctively, she threw out her arms and legs to break her fall. Screaming, falling, the carpeted stairs rose up to meet Nikki as she hurtled toward them. Her eyes briefly snagged her horrified friends watching at the bottom of the steps. Bracing for impact, Nikki scrunched into a ball. *Wham!* Her right arm crashed into the base-board and tread with a shattering crunch. The momentum of the collision angled her toward the banister and opened her tuck. *Whack!* Nikki took another tread, and another, and another. Upended, she plunged end over end, in a series of thuds and smacks until she landed crumpled, then sprawled out on her back on the entry marble floor at the base of the staircase. Nikki remained conscious.

Ben ran to call for the rescue squad as Mary knelt at her side, trying to assess her physical condition, afraid to move her.

The momentum of his fateful blow had pulled Grant down the top part of the stairs. Karl leaped over Nikki's body onto the third step to defend her from further attack.

No need, Grant dissolved into a sitting stupor on the steps, dazed by the magnitude of his anger, hunched forward, rung out, cupping his knees. Nikki's eyes caught the sun glinting on the wedding medallion swinging outside his sweater. Past him, at the top of the landing, a pallid Bridget matched the white sheet she clutched.

Absolute pain utterly racked Nikki. She tried to pick herself up, but Mary discouraged it. Like statues frozen in place, everyone maintained their positions, with the exception of Bridget. She disappeared to dress.

Soon the "ee-oo-ee-oo" of the sirens wailed up the driveway. Their lights flashed against the gray of the sky and intruded into the house. The police accompanied the rescue squad. Shortly thereafter, Bruce came. Ben had called him too. Shocked and overwhelmed at the gruesome scene, Bruce sank speechless to the marble. The police collected everybody and separated them for questioning. Loudly letting their bags of paraphernalia plop down on the marble, the medics began attending to Nikki. Their touch sent blinding pain coursing through her body. She closed her eyes.

Nikki drifted in and out of consciousness over the next few days. Along with another concussion, multiple scalp wounds, a broken right arm, and three cracked ribs, she lost the baby. Her mom and dad flew in to spend the endless hours sitting at her hospital bedside waiting for her eyes to flutter open so they could lend their support and coax her back to consciousness.

Besides the cadre of doctors, nurses, and other assorted medical personnel, a particularly affable professional in a starched lab coat and silk tie made twice-daily visits to Nicole's bedside. Never issuing any assessments or opinions, his sapphire-blue eyes intently pored over the chart at the foot of her bed. He seemed to linger a little longer over her hand while taking her pulse.

Several times Fran tried to engage him about her daughter's condition. Each time, however, with his finger to his lips in a quieting fashion, he would slightly smile and say, "There's progress," then pat Fran's hand and leave.

Mary and Karl wrote an ambiguous "accident around the house" press release for public consumption in an attempt to stem the hotbed of speculation, which swirled around the Surrey house after the rescue squad followed by a police investigation.

In their investigation of the violence, the police found pot, acid, and a plethora of other illegal substances, including cocaine, in the house. They hauled everyone present at the scene in for questioning. In deference to his notoriety, the court quietly placed Grant under house arrest and exacted an exorbitant fine for the drugs. Battery charges remained pending with the court, waiting for Nikki to be able to sign a complaint.

The incident tore poor Bruce apart. As a pacifist, he desperately wanted to be able to sweep the event under the rug and return to an idyllic life, but every fiber in his body detested Grant's actions and wanted justice to prevail. He freed Nikki, with his blessings, to exact whatever price she deemed appropriate, including ruining the career of Grant Henderson.

Almost two weeks elapsed before Nikki began to put together all the pieces and function again. Mary helped Fran find a private flat for Nikki to move into following her release from the hospital. Armfuls of flowers from her fans accompanied her home. Even after a week or two, a particularly nice bouquet of gardenias continued to arrive every Friday, just as it had while she had been hospitalized.

Nikki didn't agonize over whether to continue the marriage. Even before reading the police report, she understood that the drugs and alcohol exacerbated Grant's behavior, but she refused to dignify those facts with any consideration. Grant had broken his numerous commitments to her on multiple occasions. She wouldn't set herself up to be shredded by his Jekyll-and-Hyde personality again or to be his patsy while he played with his paramours. Grant literally had killed the only reason Nikki might have tried to work things out.

As much as her ribs hurt, the physical pain paled in comparison to her loss of the baby. It devastated Nikki. Even at the tender age of nineteen, her heart had already made the leap to motherhood. Tears and grief overwhelmed her even at the most innocuous of times. Fears of collapsing from the weight of the emotional turmoil kept her from disclosing the pregnancy or miscarriage to her fans.

Nikki contacted an astute divorce attorney, adept in handling high-profile cases. In exchange for her not pressing assault and battery charges and keeping the story of the violence out of the press, Grant agreed to buy Nikki another home in Surrey, provide her with a million-pound allotment, and restrain from maligning her in public.

Despite Fran and Mary's advice against it, Nikki wanted to go back to that house in Surrey, to clean out her things. More than collecting her possessions though, Nikki wanted to face down her demon of defeat there, rather than have it haunt her throughout all time. But Fran and Mary weren't about to let her go alone. Ironically, it was April 1 when they pulled up to the gate. A fine mist drizzled down the windshield of Mary's car. The trees, pregnant with springtime buds, prepared to burst forth in their glorious color riot of rebirth.

That day, the grass reflected its already-lush emerald color upon the wet brown trunks of the trees, as if enticing them to reawaken to life.

The three of them stood on the front stoop. No one, not even the maid, had reentered the house since the police finished their investigation. They didn't have to worry about Grant either, for he had already fled back to India following his release. Mary unlocked the door, swung it open, and stepped back to let her friend enter. Mentally preparing, Nikki told herself, *It's only your emotions playing on your mind. Everything will be the same as always. Inside the house, it will feel normal.*

Once again the grand staircase commanded their attention, but this time by emanating the depravity of evil instead of the elegance of grandeur. An audible gasp escaped from Fran as she witnessed the remnants of the tragedy that shattered her daughter. A pool of crusted, dried blood—Nikki's blood—lay at the base of the stairs on the marble floor. Bloody footprints trailed off from it where careless personnel had crossed. The cold horror of that day flooded the three. Scuffs, scratches, and gouges disfigured the mahogany panels. Fingering the panels on her way up the stairs, Nikki relived the pain anew as she visualized slamming into the walls again. A few strands of her bloodied hair remained embedded in the wood. At the top of the landing, she turned around and looked down the winding case. The emotional gravity of the scene threatened to physically pull her back down the staircase. Grabbing the banister for balance, Nikki slapped herself back to reality, then turned and headed down the hallway to the bedroom. Scrapes and dents pockmarked the hallway where her body had smashed into the walls.

Opening the door of the bedroom, the residue from the police search and the chaos of the devastated room gripped the trio. Empty drawers hung out of the dresser's carcass, trailing remains of their contents, spilling the rest onto the floor. The dismembered bed sat torn completely asunder, its mattress and box spring carelessly tossed against a window and wall. Lampshades and pictures tilted askew.

Wading through the jumble to the closet, Nikki's foot ran up against something embedded in the carpet. It was Grant's wedding medallion ground into the floor under a pile of debris. Picking it up, she turned it over and read the sappy message she had inscribed to him. It elicited a bitter chuckle. Shoving it into her pocket, she proceeded to the closet. Stripped from their hangers, all their clothes lay heaped in a pile in the middle of the floor. Nikki picked a few of her favorites from the mess, leaving the rest.

They made their way back down the stairs, past the scene, and deposited the rescued articles by the door, then headed toward the kitchen to sort through things there. It, along with the rest of the house, hung in a similar state of dishevelment. Amusingly, the empty gin bottle Nikki had found on her way through the kitchen on that fateful day still stood in its original position on the counter joined now by a host of other wreckage. Nikki wasn't prepared for the mess left in the wake of the investigation. It sapped her strength. In the end, she took nothing. She didn't want anything badly enough to slog through the emotional battle of straightening out a war zone.

Physically, they supported Nikki on her way back to the entry and out, but the feeling of forgetting something gnawed at her before Mary locked the front door. Finally, Nikki remembered—the baby clothes. Mary ran back up the stairs and returned with the still neatly packed boxes. The police had left them untouched.

Sunshine parted the rain clouds by the time Mary locked the door.

But Nikki couldn't return to the rented flat just yet, so her friend drove meandering roads into the countryside. Along the way, they passed a plain country church. Drawn to it, Nikki asked Mary to pull over.

Inside the vestibule, before entering the sanctuary, her gaze fell on the poor box. Compelled by involuntary forces, Nikki's fingers found the gold piece in her slacks. Pulling the chain and wedding medallion out of her pocket, she read it for the last time. Then she deposited the medallion like a coin through the slot. The gold disc dragged the chain along behind it as it disappeared down the hole of the box. A metallic clink gurgled up as it joined the coins at the bottom. "Good riddance. Let them melt down the gold to help some poor soul." She pushed open the chapel door with her left hand, when her gold wedding band and diamond engagement ring caught her eye. Immediately, Nikki stripped them from her finger and returned to the box. "So long, Grant," she said beneath her breath and let them fall through the open slot into the box.

Entering the sanctuary, Nikki slipped into a back pew and tried to pray. From her Christian childhood, she knew she was supposed to forgive Grant, but she couldn't erase the crazed wildness in his eyes that day. Her wounds were too fresh to pray for forgiveness. She thought about her baby, and her mind wandered to what might have been as she struggled with the loss. Nikki wanted to pray for God's guidance in her life but worried she had abused His gifts too much already to ask for anything else. Her prayers continually got tangled up with her thoughts. The picture hanging on the wall of Jesus carrying the lost lamb captured her heart. In the end, all she could do was to ask Jesus to please hold her like the recovered lamb.

CHAPTER 13

★

On Her Own

Mending her bones and ending her marriage exacted less of a toll on Nikki than the healing of her spirit. In the countless hours of bed rest, self-doubt monopolized her. She had made a bad choice for a life's partner. Besides being dazzled by all that was Grant Henderson, where had she gone wrong? Would she ever be able to trust another man again? Would she want to?

Nikki wanted to hide. And hiding included leaving the business. Even though she had never wanted a career handed to her because of Grant, in her heart she believed that was exactly what had happened. Nikki felt she had never earned her career. *Luck handed it to me. Without Grant and the Merseymen, will the fans still want me? Even though I started out a solo act, since I've been performing with the Merseymen, in the minds of my fans, am I permanently attached to them? Do I in fact have any real talent, or did the fans embrace me because of the famous four?* Nikki was afraid to ask them—she worried she might not like their answer.

She called Bruce, and without confessing her misgivings, she quit. Having been thrown off, she refused to get up out of the mud. Employing a mixture of empathy and sweet talk, Bruce tried to get Nikki back on her horse. She refused. As a last resort, he promised he'd release her from her contract if she'd do just one more chat session.

So the second week of April, Nikki gathered her nerves and sat down with a large group of fans for a chat.

Immediately, a girl from in front asked, "Are you okay now?"

"My ribs are still sore from the tumble, and I'll have my arm in the cast for another month. But other than that, I'm perfectly fit."

Another enthusiastic hand shot up. "What about singing? Will you sing again?"

"In a few weeks, when it doesn't hurt to take a breath, I promise I'll be back in front of a microphone again."

"Why didn't you go home to America to be with your parents after this accident?"

"Because *this* is my home. I didn't want to leave you all."

The room erupted with cheers and applause.

"Will you do concerts?"

"Will you tour?"

"You'll do England first, won't you?"

From the back of the room, a young male bolted up and shouted, "What about the freakin' bastard?"

Silence.

"Excuse me?" Nikki questioned. "Who might that be?"

"You know," another shot up.

"Yeah. Henderson…the lout." Another launched to his feet.

"Yeah, Grant!" More stood, adding their voices—building an undercurrent.

The room began to writhe. Bruce's eyes widened. Just what he needed—one of his pop vocalists cannibalizing the other.

Doggedly loyal, the chatters wanted blood.

Slapping her knee with her left hand, Nikki pretended to be sincerely caught up in laughter. "Oh, *that* bastard!" she sprang back. "What's the big deal?" She held up her left hand, wiggling her naked ring finger. "He's gone. Hey, he preferred someone else. And I've got all of you!"

The chatters cheered.

Seizing control, becoming "one" with them again, Nikki moved into their midst. "But seriously, can we talk? I've always been able to come to you with problems. Can we do that now? I need to let you in on a little something."

Instinctively, they drew near.

"Would you all mind if I tried this singing thing on my own for a while? I love the Merseymen dearly just like *you* do. Right?"

A hesitant nod spread through the crowd.

"Great! See, I knew that! I thought I'd like to try to sing now, just for you. Maybe it's time for me to test my wings all on my own. What do you think? Yeah?"

The eager male from the back piped up again, "Yeah! Show the lousy creep you don't need him!"

Oh, how Nikki wanted to jump on the bandwagon of that emotion! But she knew better. "No. No, you don't understand. See, I've been working on this idea even before Grant and I split. I want to do some things differently—special for you. I want to be able to get more intimate with you. It's hard to do that dragging a band of singers along with you. That doesn't mean you can't enjoy them too. Sometimes you want a party. Sometimes you want a romantic evening alone. Get it?"

Enthusiasm bubbled up from the group. The idea of Nikki again as a solo act ignited their interest. They bombarded her with ideas and directions.

The hiccup in her performance schedule and hiatus from the public eye in actuality lasted only two months—still, an eternity to be out of the limelight. Encouraged by her return chat session, as Bruce knew she would be, Nikki worked the "grass roots" to build a solid foundation of support for her solo career. Over those next four weeks, until her ribs finished healing and she could stand in front of a mic again, Nikki toured throughout London, meeting fans, mixing with them on their turf. She kept Jarred and his security staff busy full-time so she could be out and about with the people who put her on top. Nikki didn't limit herself to the cities either but also ventured out into the countryside. Her excursion to meet the fans on their terms amazed and pleased Bruce because she wasn't just skimming off the cream of fame—she was cultivating lifelong kinship with the people. Karl's photographer, Jimmy, shot her entire road tour of Britain. Karl expertly timed its release. Nikki's appeal peaked. The kids rabidly devoured everything put before them.

Feeling well enough to move out of the temporary rented flat, Nikki decided to look for her own place. She pooled her house-hunting efforts with Candy, fresh from her divorce from Jack. Within a week, they found a large, six-acre estate with a caretaker's cottage. Too immense for their single families, Candy and Nikki drew up the contract to divide the property. Candy and the baby would have the manor house and half the land while Nikki took the cottage and the remaining land. They'd share a groundskeeper. That way, the two could always keep an eye on each other, if need be.

By no means should this caretaker's cottage be construed as a shack. The two-story stucco-over-stone structure, with its push-out casement windows of diamond-shaped leaded panes of glass, afforded Nikki a large open-beamed kitchen with ample adjoining dining space. The extremely generous living room supported a massive floor-to-ceiling fieldstone fireplace at one end. Three bedrooms and a bath sprawled across the upstairs, and the surrounding gardens ran on forever.

Nikki wanted her home to envelop her in an ambiance of warmth—a kick-off-your-shoes-you're-home-now feeling. She chose a honey-maple farm-style table with captain's chairs for the dining room and a welcoming traditional overstuffed sofa and chairs with wood plank end tables for the living room. To keep an air of rusticity, Nikki spiced up the decor with a few antiques. She splashed her bedroom in soothing pink and white, from the pink-over-white wainscoted and papered walls to the white eyelet curtains and rose-toned English floral comforter.

Despite her move from the rented London flat back to Surrey, the gardenias continued to arrive every Friday, with one change. Now the florist delivered two bouquets with cards labeling them "down-stairs" and "upstairs." The fact that the flowers followed her unpublicized move led Nikki to suspect they weren't from an ordinary fan wishing her a speedy recovery. *Who has that much access to my personal life? Who got close enough to know that I now have two floors?* Still absent a sender's signature, Nikki asked Jarred to check with the florist.

The florist offered no clues as to the sender's identity. His floral arranger had discovered an envelope full of pound notes with instructions left on the arranging table one day. After Nikki's move, another envelope of cash containing her new address and more instructions appeared in the same place. Fearing a stalker, Jarred initiated a sweep of Nikki's security system and beefed up the provisions around the property. But nothing alarming developed.

In late May 1966, when her ribs had almost completely healed, Nikki tore back into the recording studio with a renewed vigor. Fresh and ready, she recorded her third solo album, *Nikki Off on Her Own.* Jimmy shot a natural-style cover photo of Nikki in boots and jeans, suede jacket slung over her shoulder, looking back at the camera while embarking down a groomed dirt road into the country. In two days, it went platinum. Bruce booked Nikki in a series of concerts opening the second week in June at the London Palladium. Within hours, the tickets sold out. For the first time since Bruce launched Nikki, he devoted the majority of his efforts to her career, probably because her sales numbers vaulted her into the number 1 position in his stable. Truly, Nikki had progressed from the enthusiastic, naive schoolgirl who almost incited a riot, to a seasoned veteran, able to read her crowd and direct them along a calculated path.

Her old studio band toured with her, providing backup. Sure, the butterflies of old also returned; but Nikki drew her energy from that marvelous preconcert dynamism, sucking up all she could get. She leaped out of the box. Nikki had returned! The unconditional, loving spirit of the audience swelled over the footlights, blanketing her with their strident affection. Answering their energy, she gave them all she had.

As she performed, she tried to make personal eye contact with every section of the audience. Crossing the first loge box, her eyes stopped on a seemingly familiar figure of great aplomb who, in a show of respect, doffed his imaginary hat to her. The bright spot-lights obscured any further recognition.

Her wave of ever-mounting popularity swept Nikki from her British concerts onto the Continent. All her free time she spent in the recording studio creating more product; she squeezed in at least two chat sessions a week. With the Merseymen, Nikki had partici-pated only on the fringes of this life. Now it swallowed her whole, pulling her into its eye. Time no longer permitted Bruce to jump on all the requests for the television shows, interviews, and perfor-mances. Nikki's career finally arrived at the place where *they* selected the shows and interviews designed to garner her the most benefit. Despite stepped-up security, a bouquet of gardenias mysteriously greeted her in each new city.

Nikki's summer tour landed in Vienna the first week of July 1966. Her stop happened to coincide with the world-class weight-lift-ing trials being held there. Lifters from all over the globe converged in the capital of Austria for the competition.

Shortly after Nikki's arrival, the junior ambassador from the United Kingdom to Austria, Howard Bates, sent a telegram seeking an audience with her. Finding nothing unusual about the inquiry, Nikki carved out an hour from her schedule as requested. She assumed he wanted to review plans for the reception for her the following night.

Bates received her in one of the salons off the main reception area of the embassy. After a terse introduction, this short man, of wiry build with glasses and a mustache, got directly down to busi-ness. "I am sure you are aware of the weight-lifting trials taking place in our city at this time."

Nikki nodded.

"We would be very obliged if you could do us a favor. We'd like it if you would publicly attend the competition tomorrow. Of course, I imagine the usual attending retinue of photographers and reporters will accompany you. Following the awards ceremony, naturally you would sign autographs. I understand the top heavyweight Russian competitor will ask you for an autograph. He will hand you a red pen to use. Rather than returning the pen, we'd like you to absentmindedly keep it after writing out his autograph, and in fact, you should continue to use it as you sign others. In all the surrounding hubbub, it wouldn't be anything out of the ordinary for you to stash the pen in your pocket, purse, or whatever." Proud of himself for spitting all that out at once, Howard Bates came up for a breath.

Fleetingly, Nikki wondered how Bates knew for certain these future events would occur, especially since they involved people from behind the Iron Curtain. Secretly she wondered, *Man, has someone set me up for some prank?*

But this wasn't a joke. Bates, even for a junior diplomat, employed too many words and had far too serious a demeanor for this to be a joke.

"Once I take the pen, what do you want me to do with it?" an incredulous Nikki asked.

"Later in the evening, as you know, both the US and British embassies are hosting a joint reception for you. Even among our ranks, you have many fans and undoubtedly will be asked to sign autographs. You should use the same pen that you took from the Russian. Ultimately Ambassador Junger's daughter will ask for an autograph. At that point, simply hand the pen from the Russian to her along with your autograph. I will see to it that you will have another pen for the next person to request an autograph.

"Of course, I can do it. But why not get the pen from the Russian yourself?"

Bates responded indignantly, "We aren't at liberty to discuss the particulars."

At that moment, a sophisticated man of regular stature in his midfifties with ample amounts of salt-and-pepper mottling in his hair joined them. "You see, Miss Moore," he advanced, his hand outstretched in welcome, "there are some international protocol matters here that concern us. Allow me to introduce myself. I'm the ambassador, Michael Junger."

Nikki shook his hand. Ambassador Junger continued as they all sat, "Mr. Bates and I operate in official capacities. In our roles as public servants, if either of us were to have contact with any person from an Eastern Bloc country without going through appropriate channels…well…it could create an international incident with a lot of fuss over such an insignificant matter as a gift. But as an international celebrity, your fame makes you a citizen of the world. For you to absentmindedly keep a pen from a Russian weight lifter in the middle of a media frenzy wouldn't raise a single eyebrow."

"Then it's a gift from the weight lifter?" Nikki tried to follow his logic.

The ambassador nodded. "Yes, for my daughter. That's right. It's just a gift. She really likes him. It will be something that she will treasure forever."

"What if someone asks for the pen back?" she questioned.

"We hope that won't happen," Bates jumped in.

Junger cut him off, "Yes, that would be a shame. My daughter is an ardent fan of weight lifter Yuri's, and she is really looking forward to having that pen from him."

As Ambassador Junger courteously escorted Nikki to the door, he whispered in her ear, "Let's keep this pen thing just between us. People could get the wrong idea about an ambassador's daughter receiving a gift from a Russian." He clucked, "Tsk, tsk, such big deals over little things."

The next afternoon came off without a hitch. Edward from her security team accompanied Nikki to the trials, which she even found compelling. Afterward, she gladly signed autographs and posed for pictures with the athletes and audience members. Neither Karl nor Nikki could believe the unusually large number of press in attendance at a sporting event, all of whom seemed so enamored with Nikki's appearance.

Face-to-face with the Russian weight lifter, his size amazed Nikki. She hardly came to his shoulders. Her hips were the size of just one of his thighs. But she found him the quintessential cliché of a cuddly teddy bear—soft-spoken and gentle. In heavily accented

English, he said, "I am big fan of yours," as he handed her a piece of paper and the red pen.

"Really! Where do you hear my music?"

"My girlfriend is skater. She uses your music for skating. I don't understand all words, but I like your voice." He pushed out a humble smile as he lowered his head. *"Das vadanya,"* he said modestly, before others shoved in front of him for a turn.

As instructed, Nikki finished out the session using the red pen then dropped it into her purse and headed to the hotel to prepare for the evening's festivities. With children in attendance, she chose a high-necked, sleeveless empire gown of mint pastel taffeta, trimmed with seed pearls. Piling her long tresses in curls atop her head, she finished the ensemble off with drop pearl earrings.

Floating through the party, Nikki mingled with the various dignitaries, with their wives, and with the captains of industry from all three countries. The room smelled of expensive perfume, roses, and power. Despite having to work, she loved these white-tie galas. It touched her that the British ambassador and his charming wife remembered her from another ball at the foreign secretary's office in London.

Eventually, the time came for Nikki to get out the pen to sign autographs and pose for pictures. Ambassador Junger brought his daughter Kari forward. Proudly, she presented her autograph book. They chatted for a few moments, then Nikki signed between the pages where John Lennon in '64 and Elvis in '65 had signed. Handing Kari the pen along with her book, Nikki smiled. She knew what a special feeling it must be to get such a long-awaited souvenir. Nikki's eyes followed her as she stepped back among the crowd to her father's side. Nikki continued to watch her. She wanted to see Kari's excitement and gratitude. *No doubt her reaction will please her father, after all the silly nonsense he went through to get her that souvenir.*

Mechanically, Nikki accepted another book to sign, but something seemed off as she continued to observe those two. Kari never acknowledged the pen. And she didn't keep it! Passing it to her father, she shuffled off. She never reveled in possessing the anticipated treasured writing instrument, even for a brief moment.

Insistence of the next in line snapped Nikki back to reality. With a boy's book in hand to sign, now she needed a pen.

True to the ambassador's word, a pen materialized before her—gold, shining in the evening's light. Nikki looked up to thank the bearer, right into the dancing eyes of the mysterious man from Naples. "The lovely lady seems to be without a pen. May I offer mine?"

Nikki signed, then handed the book back to the young lad.

Immediately, she turned back to the man, anxious to finally make his acquaintance once and for all.

She turned back to vapors.

Hot commitments across the Continent ate up the summer. Pressure from Asia, Japan, and Hong Kong mounted. Bruce planned to open those markets near the end of the year. If all went well, they'd do the United States in a winter tour, hopefully in February like the Merseymen—for luck.

Before long, a common theme of "suitors" for Nikki emerged in the chat sessions. The press wildly speculated about her love life. Nikki tried the old saw "I have all of you." While the fans at the sessions swallowed it, the press nagged. Gun-shy, Nikki had relegated men and dating to the basement of her priorities. In reality, her line about the fans proved to be more truth than poetry.

While Bruce appreciated her relentless dedication to her career, part of a luminary's success centers around the ability to exude a sexual presence—the sizzle that sells—by teasing availability. Begrudgingly, she complied. Nikki discovered "seen dating." Devoid of romantic entanglements, each person uses the other to be "seen with," thereby enhancing his/her own status. And before long, she made the scene with this sensational pop artist at a disco and dined with that hot rising star at the restaurant *du jour*. Cameras caught them, the tabloids tattled on them, and once again, the entertainment world blissfully rotated on its own axis. Unwilling to risk emotional involvement, the practice provided a totally benign way to date, unless someone believed the press being generated. Rigidly, she avoided dating anyone outside the business. They proved to be too vulnerable to the siren of celebrity, easily mistaking their fantasies for love. An expert on this subject, Nikki had gained her experience at Grant's invitation.

Nikki kept up the grueling concert/recording pace through the summer into fall. In between the Australian tour and the Asian trip, Bruce carved out two weeks away from the road for Nikki, then just as craftily encumbered them. "How about doing a Christmas special? I snagged a deal for a seventeen-country special to air the third week in December. The producers want your typical Christmas on the farm in America. Think your parents would open up *Creekside*? We'll give 'em the whole squishy production—snow, carolers, decorations up the...well you know. What ya say, luv? Ya up for it?"

After being with Bruce for over two years, Nikki knew he had already inked the deal. "Asking" was just his way of breaking the news to her. If Fran and Richard refused their farm, Bruce would rent one!

As Christmas specials go, the November shoot sliced production time to the bone—as most are usually shot in August/September. Consequently, Nikki cut the accompanying Christmas soundtrack album at Reading's Kutztown Road recording studio with hired musicians and vocalists. Meanwhile, set decorators blanketed everything at *Creekside* with swaths of red and green, twinkle lights, and fake snow! For the album cover and exteriors on the special, they "borrowed" another farm in a neighboring county to keep fans from invading the Moores' privacy.

As the last plastic snowflake disappeared into the production cleanup's vacuum, Nikki departed for her tour of Asia. Eighteen hours later, Nikki deplaned to greet a crowd of over twenty thousand! Stepping out onto a platform equipped with microphones and Japanese dignitaries, a roar rose up when she bowed to the welcoming party. Pulling out her small vocabulary of Japanese from a previous visit, she called out to the thousands hanging off the rails of the airport, *"Konnichiwa!"* A thunderous cheer returned her greeting. The city ambassadors presented her with the equivalent of the key to the city. *"Arigato, arigato!"* Nikki thanked them in Japanese.

The insatiable Japanese devoured all her waking moments from her shopping excursions to her learning to skillfully operate the tricky chopsticks. She dined sitting on the floor and never squirmed when served plates of raw fish so fresh it flopped on the plate before her. Accelerating into hyperdrive, Nikki's troupe used the energy of that trip to psych themselves up for the approaching tour of the States in February.

By the first week of December, they were within hours of releasing their initial barrage of records and media hype onto the American market. Bruce picked December 12 as Nikki's debut day. All of them felt the tension rising as they stared into the abyss—"the American market." The capricious taste of the States could put Nikki literally on top of the world or break her in two. A single hit on the charts there didn't ensure success. "One-hit wonders" bought nothing. Failure in the States could poison every other market Nikki had previously conquered. But the allure of the golden promised land shimmered and danced too seductively to be ignored.

On December 7, Nikki returned to her hotel suite to find a dour Bruce and Karl with a nearly empty bottle of scotch on the coffee table. *The Sullivan Show* had postponed Nikki's appearance in February till the following September. It wasn't a fatal blow, but close. Hundreds of thousands of dollars tied up in promotion packages waited in warehouses in the States, now without a vehicle to launch them. The duo feared the impression this would make, since in the entertainment business, perception *is* reality. Sitting down with Nikki, they put their heads together. Finally, it was decided that they'd spin a tale that Nikki's career was too hot to take time to "do America" just then. Bruce would overbook her and make it look like *they* put the Sullivan people off until fall. Footage of exuberant Japan and a movie deal or two would certainly bolster the premise. This approach doubled Nikki's already-hectic schedule but neatly solved the situation. They packed for two days in Seoul with a final week in Hong Kong.

The Harbour City—Marketplace of the World—offered significantly more than a concert stop and shopping respite from a frenzied schedule. It would change Nicole Moore's life forever.

CHAPTER 14

★

High Tea and Espionage

Ⓔast quite literally meets West in the British colony of Hong Kong on the other side of the world. On any given corner, one could routinely pause for tea while overlooking a stock of Chinese chickens hanging upside down in the adjacent storefront. Almost everyone spoke British-accented English. Familiar red double-decker buses lumbered up and down the streets just as in London. Even the round postboxes and square red phone booths mimicked those in the UK. But a person could never mistake the colony for the motherland. Hong Kong moved with people, people, and more people, who choked the thoroughfares throughout the province, then spilled out into the water. Locked in by water, with Communist China breathing down the throat of the adjoining Kowloon Peninsula, buildings had no place to go other than up. Ever-increasing tall fingers of concrete, steel, and glass stretched toward the sky.

A duty-free port, ships from all over the world off-loaded in Hong Kong, serving up a virtual shopper's paradise. All countries traded in this marketplace of the world. It wasn't unusual for a Soviet ship flying the hammer and sickle to pull into port. With Communism being the "Red Menace," this pariah so blatantly sitting in the harbor only increased the intrigue and mystery Nikki felt pulsing through its veins. It seemed as if everyone engaged in some form of free enterprise. Both on the island of Hong Kong and the peninsula of Kowloon, stores of every kind crawled up into the skyscrapers' vast towers of merchandise. Independent vendors filled the sidewalks in front of the stores, up stairways, and along back alleys, peddling their goods from pushcarts, portable display cases, or even simple cloths. Local merchants constantly bombarded people in the street with their sales pitches, trying to lure them to their merchandise. Vendors expected customers to haggle. The streets of Hong Kong offered everything imaginable, legal as well as illegal.

Nikki's Hong Kong schedule included one concert, two televised interviews, and three chat sessions. She arrived at the hotel to find an invitation to the governor's mansion for a private audience at high tea the next day. Since the British governing authority for the colony emanated from the Governor's office, the invitation required significant deference.

The conservative British tradition of high tea at four in the afternoon demanded appropriate attire. Nothing "Nikki" would do. A quick trip to the clothier in one of the shops on the hotel's ground floor provided an appropriate business suit in gray with a white blouse. The colorful Hermes scarf from the adjoining store added just enough pizzazz. A fashionable twist got her hair up off her shoulders. Nikki knew Governor Albert Brown and his wife, Ruth, from the foreign minister's office. They had hosted a reception for her before at the registry office in London. Usually high tea with the governor, despite the wording "private audience," meant other notables would be in attendance. Nikki supposed, since Governor Brown would be retiring at the end of the month, his replacement might be also present.

Arriving several minutes prior to the hour, Mrs. Brown greeted Nikki, then graciously ushered her into the parlor. The gentlemen were yet to arrive. Soon a reserved woman in her forties joined them. Mrs. Brown introduced her as Mary James, wife of the incoming governor. Mrs. Brown poured. It seemed only the women would partake of tea. They chatted quite politely over finger sandwiches and tea for more than a half hour. Both quizzed Nikki about the harried pace the tabloids painted of her life and wanted to know the latest about the pop idols she had been seen dating.

At quarter to the hour, the doors to the parlor parted, and the governor walked in accompanied by two other men. Abruptly, the women terminated their conversations with regrets and left. A servant cleared, while the governor introduced Nikki to his replacement, Nigel James, a man in his midforties and quite buttoned down to business. Neither, however, moved to introduce a third rather rumpled gentleman. Before departing, the butler decanted a bottle of sherry, pouring four glasses. With an underscoring finality, he slid the doors shut behind him.

Governor Brown made a few pleasant remarks as he distributed the sherry. He still made no attempt to introduce the stranger. Quite traditionally, they raised their glasses in a toast to the queen. Following that, the governor began with a sputter. "Miss Moore, we would like you to know how grateful we are for the service you provided..."

Nikki used his hesitation as an opportunity to put him at ease. "Please, call me Nikki. And, sir, to what service are you referring?"

Then Mr. James interrupted, stabbing at conversation, "Miss Moore, your career seems to be going rather nicely right now, doesn't it?"

Letting them lead, Nikki smiled hesitantly at the dubious direction of their discourse.

Mr. James continued, "Yes, well, my point is that you have made a comfortable living from the British populace and..."

The rumpled stranger with close-cropped salt-and-pepper brown hair and brown eyes noticeably shifted his position in his chair.

Mr. James fumbled on. "I suppose you enjoy the work. You do, don't you? Meeting all the people, traveling all over the world?"

The stranger mumbled some disgruntlement, drawing their attention. He pulled a cigarette case from the breast pocket of his brown suit. "Mind if I smoke?" he asked in his gravelly voice.

"Care to join me, Miss Moore?" He emphasized her name.

Politely, she refused.

His voice betrayed his Bronx lineage.

The governor scurried to find an ashtray while Mr. James tried to find his place.

"Judas priest! You guys are pussyfooting all around the issue." The American bolted from his chair, paced the room, then pulled

147

up a seat directly across from the singer. "Miss Moore, let's talk." He stuck his cigarette in his lips. It bobbed up and down while he spoke. "Oh, by the way, I'm Bob Mann." He put his hand out for her to shake and shook hers generously. "Now here's the deal. Remember in Vienna you met a guy named Junger?"

"Yes, the ambassador," Nikki added.

"Okay. And he asked you to get a pen from a Russian weight lifter."

"Yes. For his daughter."

"Yeah, whatever. Well, that wasn't just any pen."

"Ahem!" The governor obviously cleared his throat.

"Okay!" Mann threw back at him. "Okay."

Then back to Nikki, "Anyway, you helped us out."

"And you are...?" she led.

"We are a conglomeration from the CIA, the NSA, MI5, along with NATO, SEATO, and a few other alphabet soup organizations."

Nikki almost fell over. She looked to the governor and Mr. James for confirmation.

Stoically British, their poker faces offered no clues.

"The point is you helped us out in a big way. And because you are this tremendous rock star and travel all over the world and meet everybody, we could really use your services."

Wanting to make sure she grasped his meaning, she started, "You mean—"

Mann jumped back in, "You can go places without question that would take us weeks of maneuvering to accomplish, not to mention the risk to lives and drain on manpower."

"Mr. Mann, I find it impossible to believe that I can do things your organization can't."

"Your notoriety together with your celebrity status essentially makes you a citizen of the world. That gives you unlimited access to a vast amount of different people, locations around the globe, and all sorts of contacts."

There was that term again "citizen of the world." The reiteration of it caught her attention but she saw his point.

"You're a smart chick. In the back of your mind, you must be putting together that pen scheme. Yeah, we used you as a courier."

He was right. Nikki was piecing it together.

"The Russki passed you some vital information, and neither you nor the world were any the wiser. Your security guy never even picked up on it! We probably could pull this pen thing off a couple dozen times. In fact, even when you aren't working for us, you should make a habit of stashing a few pens, just to establish a pattern."

"Wait a minute, Mr. Mann. What do you mean work for you?"

"Oh, wasn't I clear? I'm here to recruit you for service to your country."

Again, Nikki looked to the governor or Mr. James for verification or rescue. Silently, they had disappeared from the room.

Several emotions washed over her in rapid succession. First came disbelief. *It couldn't be they want me.* Then ego inflation combined with a momentary delusion of grandeur. *Wow, they do want me!* Mann's pitch obliterated any thought of caution.

Catching Nikki eyeing the bait, Mann set the hook. "This is something only *you* can do for us. Your country would be indebted to you for your service. Right now we are waging two costly wars on diverse fronts. Obviously the one in Vietnam, but just as crucial, the Cold War for supremacy in the West."

Fidgeting with her glass of sherry, Nikki mulled it over. His flattering flag-waving preempted her own logical dissemination of his proposal.

Mann played his lure. "It won't require anything extra of you. We'll have you attending some first-class parties to pass on the little trinkets you collect for us." He made it all sound so innocuous.

At that point, for the drama of it, Nikki almost considered asking for a cigarette while she pondered his proposition. It fit the character of the moment.

"What do you think, Miss Moore?" Mann pressured. "Are you in?"

Although in a state of shock, she managed a few questions. "What about danger? Is this going to put either my people or me in harm's way?"

"Were you in any danger at the weight-lifting trials? Did any-one throw a pass you couldn't handle?" he cracked.

She rebuked him for his smart-aleck answer, "What if I want out? Is this like the military where I'm locked in? What if I refuse a request?"

"If you refuse, you refuse. It's no big deal. If we really need your services, we'll try to persuade you, but ultimately the final decision always rests with you. You're never under any obligation. We're not the military. You're a civilian, at liberty to participate or not. So will you do it?"

"Can I take some time to think this over?"

"Sure. Take a few minutes. But the sooner we have your answer, the sooner we can proceed. We have a job waiting for you." Mann tightened the screws.

In the abbreviated time given her, Nikki failed to notice how cleverly Mann had skirted the issue of danger. Chalk another one up to being a virgin in the woods.

Prodded by Mann's fingers impatiently drumming on the chair, she said, "Yes."

"Great!"

"Do I have to sign anything or take an oath?" She imagined some sort of initiation was needed to bring her into their service. *There has to be more to it than this*, she thought.

"Nope. Just express a willingness to help, which you did." Mann glossed it over.

"I guess now you will run a security check on me for—"

"Schweetie," Mann replied sarcastically with yet another ciga-rette dangling from his lip. "We already did that, way before we ever contacted you in Austria. Initially I'll be your contact. Now"—Mann rubbed his hands together—"how about going shopping?"

"Sure. That sounds great," she answered, eager to explore the possibilities.

"In between your shows tomorrow"—he pulled an envelope out of his other breast pocket, revealing some US dollars, and tossed it across the table to her—"we want you to go shopping. Use the envelope. Go to the Mao shops, I mean the Chinese Crafts Store in

Kowloon. Shop all you want. Your contact will be an older Chinese woman with glasses on a chain around her neck in the fur department. You'll be looking for a blue fox coat. Pick any coat that you like. But be sure to remark to the woman that you want it to wear to go skiing in St. Moritz this winter. Leave it there to have your initials embroidered into the lining. You'll go back the next day for a final fitting and to inspect the embroidery. Then have it shipped to your home in Surrey. See, simple! Nothing out of the ordinary, and you get a free fox coat in the deal! You can even keep the change."

"I assume there will be something in the coat."

"Why not let us worry about that."

"If it's shipped to Surrey, how will you get it? Are you going to send an agent to break into my house and steal it?" Nikki started to balk.

"Lady, you watch too many movies. When it arrives, have your maid, Hannah, take it to Harrods for cold storage until you need it. Once again, nothing out of the ordinary."

"Should she see anyone in particular?"

"Nope. But to protect the fur against theft from an overzealous fan, what name would you leave it under? Obviously you wouldn't leave a ticket with 'NIKKI' splashed all over it."

"No, I'd use my middle and last names as a disguise, 'Verna, Verna Moore.'"

"Then use it here. When she picks it up later for you, the exact same coat will be waiting." He threw back a swallow of sherry, then exhaled a cloud of smoke. "Hey, just be natural with this thing. If you shop alone, fine. If you want to take a friend or a party of people, fine. Photographers, great! Just relax. Be yourself. You can't screw this thing up."

Nikki picked up the envelope and repeated, "Older woman, glasses on a chain, skiing in St. Moritz." The rumpled stranger's foreknowledge of her maid's name, where she lived, and even where she shopped totally slipped by her.

"You got it!" Mann said with a click of his tongue and a wink.

"Then I guess I'll be seeing you around." She snapped the envelope in a self-assured way, stuffed it in her purse, and turned to leave.

"Hey, Miss Moore!" Mann snagged her. "I don't have to remind ya that this is all top secret, and you can't tell anyone about this. Not Bruce, not Mary, not your mom or dad. Right?"

"That, Mr. Mann, goes without saying." With a wink, she slid out the door.

As Nikki's limo pulled away from the governor's compound, a strange feeling came over her. She felt cocky, yet uneasy, like maybe she had just been conned. *But what could it hurt?* she argued with herself. *I'll be in control. And I can call it off at any time.* Still, it bothered her that the Agency ran a security check on her without her knowledge. *Now* she noticed how freely Mr. Mann listed the people closest to her. *Why didn't I ask to see his credentials? I don't even know exactly whether I'll be working for the US or the UK.* Throwing caution to the wind, Nikki decided to push those nagging feelings out of her mind.

In a window of four hours between shows, Nikki took Mary shopping with her when she made her contact the next day. To throw off suspicion, Nikki stopped at several other stores in Kowloon before entering the Mao shop. Together, the pair ogled the jewelry downstairs. Mary bought a ring. Upstairs, Nikki purchased some embroidered table linens for her mother and some vibrant cerise Thai silk to take back to Vada. Eventually, with her heart in her throat, Nikki, with Mary in tow, wandered over to the fur department. The older woman with her glasses on a chain indeed stepped up to wait on them.

Mary chided Nikki for looking at furs—a perfect setup.

"I'm taking time to go skiing this winter. And I don't have an evening coat."

Enlisting the advice of the Chinese salesclerk, Nikki asked, "Wouldn't this be perfect to wear after skiing, when I go to St. Moritz this winter?"

Of course she agreed. With the salesclerk/contact's help, Nikki hunted for the right style of blue fox. Selecting block-style letters to be embroidered inside, she completed the sale.

Nikki had to hand it to Mann; it was incredibly simple. But she wouldn't totally breathe a sigh of relief until the coat hung in her closet later that winter. As expected, everything came off without a hitch. Empowered, during the chat session, just for kicks, Nikki snagged two pens.

On Sunday, the eighteenth of December, as Nikki walked along the shops on the island of Hong Kong, the winter sun shone brilliantly as it played in the sapphire sky among the puffy white clouds—a perfect day to be out. Nikki tapped Jarred for a security detail for her shopping trip. Since the incident in Buenos Aires, a team of at least two always followed her at a reasonable distance.

On a whim, Nikki decided she wanted to purchase a ruby that she'd have made into a pendant. Nikki couldn't get over the amount of jewelry for sale in Hong Kong. A profusion of precious stones glutted the marketplace—loose stones, mounted stones, stones the size of a speck, stones larger than marbles, stones in stores, stones on the street, stones by the handful. After a while, they lost their meaning and became "red ones, blue ones, green ones, or white ones."

Nikki started with the shops along Causeway Bay, at Kwan's Wholesale Gems. While she hovered over the display cases discussing his wares with Mr. Kwan himself, a prying jewelry shop merchant from next door stood listening at Kwan's door. Eavesdropping on her conversation with Kwan, the meddling merchant ran next door into his store, then returned clutching a small velvet bag.

Loudly, he called to Nikki from the sidewalk just outside the door, "No good quality here! No good! I have better. Lower overhead. Lower prices. Me, missy. Me. I have it. I have what you want... at cheaper price. Come see! Come see!"

Mr. Kwan cut loose with a tirade in Chinese to dismiss the meddling merchant.

But the merchant insisted harder, "Poor quality. Here, I have better. I have *a deal for you!*"

His persistence lured Nikki out of the shop and into the adjoining store.

Behind her, Nikki heard Kwan cussing out the merchant. Intent on the thrill of the hunt, "better for cheaper" pulled her out of the store.

Leading her into his store, the merchant huddled together with her, their backs to the teeming masses outside on the sidewalk. Ceremoniously, he brought forth the velvet sack again and opened it.

Carefully, as if its magnificence could only be grasped in tiny increments, he slowly revealed a dazzling red stone. Its rich color rivaled that of a fine vintage wine. The intense spotlights in his shop set fire to its facets, releasing its deep smoldering fire.

Nikki felt the breath catch in her throat.

"You like it?" he wheedled.

Mesmerized, she nodded.

"Missy want to buy it?" he prompted, moving it slowly in his hand, letting the light dance across each facet, drawing her in, seducing her.

Entranced by its beauty, again Nikki nodded. "How much?" she asked like an addict seeking a fix, too captivated to really care what price he named.

At that precise moment, a hand reached in between the two of them and plucked the stone from the merchant's hands. Horrified that someone stole her stone from in front of her, Nikki's eyes immediately followed the arm up to the man's face. The brilliant sun beaming through the window behind him obscured his identity as his hand held her stone in front of him. He studied the stone in the sun's light, reached into the breast pocket of his blazer, pulled out a jeweler's loupe, and fixed it in his eye.

Both the merchant and Nikki stood aghast at the intruder's boldness.

Finished, he removed the loupe from his eye and dropped the stone back into the merchant's hand. "Go ahead tell the lady how much you're going to charge her for that worthless piece of glass," the stranger chided.

The Chinese merchant sputtered protests. "This stone priceless—"

"Worthless is more like it!" the stranger whispered in an aside to Nikki, then came back in a clear voice. "Ah, but for you, Princess, you can have it for a mere…" He paused to let the vendor name his price.

Purposely, the stranger shifted his position, letting the sun highlight his features, revealing his identity.

Amazement popped Nikki's eyes open. "It's you," she breathed.

CHAPTER 15

★

Alexander

Nikki's eyes locked on the stranger's eyes. A hint of merriment danced in his profound blue pools. He met her gaze and held her there for a moment. "If you would permit me"—he gestured toward the stone—"I have more than a nodding acquaintance with gems. Might I be of some assistance?"

Blindsided by his surprise intrusion, Nikki nodded.

"Now, my good man," he started by putting his hand on the merchant's back, indicating to the vendor that the players in the game had changed.

The Chinese merchant continued spewing his testimonials about the quality and the incredible deal.

Finally, the stranger interrupted the merchant's endless discourse. "How much were you going to charge this lovely lady, whose own fire far outstrips your poor piece?"

Nikki acknowledged the compliment with an arch of her eyebrows.

Realizing further huckstering to be overkill, the vendor moved to close the deal. "Seven hundred dollars—US."

"What? You're insane! For this piece of paste! You'll take seven Hong Kong dollars, and I won't call the police," the intruder scoffed.

Clearly insulted, the merchant faced off with the intruder, braying at the top of his voice and rising up on his toes in an effort to negate the accusations.

Maintaining his cool demeanor, the stranger put up his hands to calm the angry merchant. "Okay. Okay. I'll settle this once and for all. You swear your stone is genuine. And I know it's worthless. I propose a small wager. If it's real, I'll pay you twice your asking price."

"In cash? US? Okay! I make bet." The merchant's eyes gleamed.

"But if it's a fake..." The stranger's words dangled in the air as he placed the stone on the shop floor. Nikki's eyes widened as she watched him put the heel of his leather loafer over the stone. Amazed, the merchant also stood frozen. The heel went up slightly and came down with a shatter. Only shards of red and white powder remained where moments earlier the faceted jewel winked up at them from the floor.

"Get out, get out!" the merchant screeched, disappearing into his back room.

"How, how did you know?" Nikki questioned as they left the shop.

"It's my business. That was an exceptional piece of paste, but paste nonetheless." His eyes sparkled as he indulged himself for a moment to observe her. "Where are my manners? Please allow me to introduce myself. I am Alexander Vincente... Alex."

Nikki immediately extended her right hand. "Hi. I'm—"

"An angel from heaven... Miss Nicole Moore... Nikki," he finished for her, taking her hand in his. "I know who you are. I confess to being a fan," he said as he looked up from a bow, hovering over her hand that he prepared to kiss. *Enchante, mademoiselle,"* he purred smoothly as he again met her gaze.

A schoolgirl, embarrassed hint of a twitter escaped from her. Nikki had only witnessed such gallantry on the silver screen. Acknowledging his chivalry with a slight curtsy, Nikki hoped to cover up any residual clumsiness on her part. However, she got the distinct impression the inveterate gentleman saw through her masquerade, and it amused him.

Alex lingered over her hand for a moment more.

"We've met before, if I'm not mistaken, Mr. Vincente. I believe I saw you for the first time in Naples."

"I'm honored." He bowed slightly from the waist. "You *were* paying attention after all. Please call me Alex. So are you really shopping for a ruby or merely toying with the local merchants?" he asked, initiating a stroll down the sidewalk.

Nikki didn't want to admit that she used her gem shopping as an excuse for adventure. "No. No, I'd really like to find a ruby to have made into a necklace."

"Then may I offer my assistance in pursuit of your quest? I know a few places."

"I'd be delighted." Nikki found his debonair sophistication engaging. Taking a moment, she filled in her security team on the details. Amid their protests, she dismissed them for the afternoon.

Alexander crooked his arm, offering it to her. Slipping her hand through his arm, she followed his lead. "There are a few good shops on the Kowloon side. Let's catch a boat across the bay." They swung onto a double-decker for the ride to the ferry tie-up.

At the docks, Alex gestured, presenting an array of choices for her. "There is a bevy of private boats, or if you are adventurous, there is always the reliable Star Ferry."

"I choose adventure." She smiled as they made their way down the gangway.

On the ferry ride to Kowloon, Nikki leaned against the rail, letting the breeze comb through her hair, while Alex chose a closed-back bench backed into a corner. In doing so, he tossed a mild caution toward her, "If you have anything of value, the warning stenciled on the pillars about pickpockets isn't just for decoration."

On his caveat, she joined him in his seat.

He smiled. "Besides, since you dismissed your security, I am responsible for you." His eyes danced as he changed the subject. "Now, Nicole, what kind of stone did you have in mind?"

"Actually, Alex, I must confess, I was chasing a bargain—the thrill of the hunt, you know, plucking a gem from the shysters of Hong Kong's back alleys. Although my father deals in precious gems, I wanted to do this on my own. But I really would like a nice ruby, deep red, about the size of my fingernail."

"How unlucky for you, you ran into the tag team of the Kwan brothers. I'm afraid they set you up. The brother in one storefront hooks your attention with some nice-quality but relatively expensive stones. If he feels he's losing the sale, he signals his brother in the adjoining store. His brother lures the pigeon out of the store with a 'steal' of a deal. A near riot ensues, and unfortunately in the confusion and haste to get the steal, the buyer assumes the substitute stone is of the same quality. The pigeon never really gets a good look at his wares."

"I'm surprised the second merchant let you get involved," Nikki commented.

"What choice did he have? He could either go along and hope my bravado was more ego than knowledge or close down the sting. This time he lost. You see, Hong Kong's alleys can pluck back."

"You're familiar with the Kwan brothers?"

"When you play in a sandbox long enough, you get to know the players. Despite its multitudes, Hong Kong is a small island. If you want to survive, you learn. In Kowloon, I have a longtime business associate named Charlie Soo. He owes me several favors. I thought we would pay him a visit."

Nikki figured they'd find Mr. Soo ensconced in a jewelry store of some repute. Imagine her surprise when they walked into an upscale porcelain emporium just off the main thoroughfare. Alexander left her to browse among the large Chinese urns while he sought out his friend. The time afforded Nikki the opportunity to visually sum him up. Obviously he had availed himself of that privilege with her on several occasions. She watched him greet his friend. She assumed Alex to be in his midthirties, at least six-foot-two. The store spotlights highlighted the gold streaks in his precisely trimmed sandy hair. And what a tan he had, even in mid-December! Impeccably dressed, his custom-tailored clothes hugged his taut contours. Wrinkles didn't dare mar his attire. But the aura he exuded transcended his physical attributes. She had never met a man who wore self-assurance so nobly or so comfortably, like a pair of fine leather loafers.

While Alex and Charlie caught up on old times, Nikki pretended interest in the brightly colored vases and figurines. Not being at all familiar with the Chinese culture, she couldn't fully appreciate the priceless art surrounding her. Eventually, the two found her. Alex made the introductions.

Mr. Soo, dressed in a cosmopolitan gray suit with a thin black tie, shook her hand with cool politeness, then made a slight bow and bade them to follow him into the back room. They edged past stacks of wooden packing crates to a secluded wrought iron table with chairs. Soo pulled the chain switching on the hanging lamp above the table. The metal lampshade funneled all the light directly onto the table. Alex and Nikki sat while the porcelain dealer disappeared. Alex easily draped his arm over the back of his chair. To thwart her internal nerves, instinctively, Nikki reverted to her proper upbringing. Sitting up correctly, she neatly folded her hands in her lap. In Soo's absence, they didn't speak.

Soon Charlie Soo reemerged and drew a small pearl-gray velvet cloth from the breast pocket of his suit. He laid it in the palm of his hand, peeled back the folds of the cloth, and exposed five large deeply colored rubies of various shapes. Their fire ignited in the light of the lone bulb. Laying the cloth with stones on it before Alexander, he offered him a jeweler's loupe then took his seat at the table.

Alexander inspected each ruby. "Charlie, these are all great specimens," he said after he finished his examination, putting the loupe to rest on the velvet. Then he slid the entire package in front of Nikki.

Carefully, she considered her actions before making a move. Her surroundings intimidated her. Acutely aware of the age difference between Alex and her, Nikki didn't want to appear to be a juvenile or a flighty female devoid of class. Refraining from any emotional exclamations, she kept a business sense about her. Individually, she moved each gem into the light to get an idea of color and fire, then returned each to its place as she finished with it. Finally, she addressed the gentlemen. "Yes, Mr. Soo, I agree these stones are exquisite. However, I am particularly fond of this one." Nikki singled out the pear-shaped ruby and let the light play on its facets.

"Perhaps you would like to examine it with the loupe?" Alex prompted.

Assured, she politely smiled. "There's really no need. Mr. Soo is a trusted friend. He wouldn't dream of trespassing on your relationship with inferior quality. And you have inspected them and given your seal of approval. I presume on your expertise."

Then Nikki addressed the Chinese shop owner. "Mr. Soo, if you're willing to part with this ruby, I would be delighted to buy it."

Smiling, Charlie Soo nodded. "Please come with me, while I prepare the stone for you." Nikki followed the two gentlemen out of the storeroom. At the front counter, Charlie folded the ruby up in its own square piece of velvet and placed it in an embroidered satin bag, which he slid toward her.

Nikki halted its progress. "Mr. Soo, I haven't paid for it yet."

Using his eyes, Soo motioned toward his friend with a confirming smile. "Mr. Alexander has taken care of it."

Nikki smiled politely then lowered her voice, to elicit confidentiality. "Mr. Soo, I only just met Mr. Vincente this afternoon. I could not accept such an extravagant gift from him at this time. I am sure you understand."

Returning her confidence with a nod and a smile, he never sought Alexander's consent. "Of course. I will prepare the bill for you."

Nikki's attention shifted back to Alexander. He stood back, arms folded, regarding her with bemusement, shaking his head. "You never even asked the price. How do you know you can afford it?"

"With multiple platinum singles and platinum albums, if I can't afford it, I'd better change managers. Besides, when you brought me here to deal with your friend, what was I going to do, haggle over the price? The sale was consummated the moment my foot crossed the threshold. The only questions to be answered were did I like what I saw? And which one would I pick?"

Alex smilingly picked up her hand and kissed it. "Amazing! Just amazing! Will you at least allow me to have the ruby mounted in a pendant setting for you?"

"Nothing extravagant," she admonished.

He acquiesced, "Simple, elegant, I promise. Something to complement your style." He kissed her hand again and took the satin sac from her.

Mr. Soo returned with the bill of sale, and Nikki counted out seven one-hundred-dollar bills to him. With business concluded, he engagingly offered her his arm for a tour of his shop. As they strolled among the porcelain, he described the history and value of his most prized pieces. Contentedly, Alexander tagged along behind. Upon completion of the tour, Mr. Soo turned to her. "My dear Miss Nicole, you would honor me if you would choose something from my humble collection. My gift to you."

In a blush, Nikki thanked him for his kindness. Thoughtfully, she considered her selection. Certainly, she didn't want to be greedy, stripping him of one of his priceless pieces, but she knew her choice had to demonstrate the appropriate appreciation and not insult his time or his offer by choosing something insignificant. Nikki decided on a medium-sized blue-and-white ginger jar, then silently checked her choice with Alex. Surreptitiously, he nodded his concurrence. Mr. Soo made arrangements to send it directly to Nikki's Surrey cottage.

Departing his shop, Nikki offered Mr. Soo her hand to shake. Once again he bowed. Nikki returned his bow. "Thank you so very much, Mr. Soo."

"Please," he said with a wink, "call me Charlie. All my friends do."

Once out on the street and well on their way from Soo's shop, Alex exclaimed, "You really impressed ol' Charlie. I have never seen him fuss over anyone so."

Nikki met his compliment with a self-conscious shrug of her shoulders.

"And me too, I might add," Alex continued. "I find myself captivated by your *savoir vivre*, enrapt and under your spell. I would be delighted if you would do me the distinct honor of letting me take you to dinner." With his Continental flair, he turned foreign phrases as easily as some people turned pages.

Instinctively, Nikki glanced at her watch, then hedged. "It's four now. I had better head back to the hotel. I really have a lot to do. Tomorrow—"

"Is another day," he persisted. "May I pick you up tonight for dinner? I know a charming little place…"

Nikki's mind raced. *What am I setting myself up for? I certainly don't want any entanglements. But this man, he's so intriguing.* Before she knew it, "I'll be ready at eight" slipped out.

Alex escorted her to her hotel's elevator. Waiting for the car, Nikki casually asked, "What should I wear?"

Alex stalled his answer until she stepped inside. Then, as the doors slid shut, his answer came. "You will be beautiful in whatever you choose."

What kind of answer was that? she wondered. In her room, Nikki agonized over the proper attire for the appropriate place. Alex lent no hint where they would be going. Nikki couldn't imagine a man of Alexander's refinement taking her to any place jean-casual. After laying out her entire closet, she decided on a strapless blue-green, polished silk sheath and matching Chinese jacket with satin frog closures at the throat. For a touch of class, she added matching satin gloves.

As Nikki prepared for the evening, her mind retraced the day. Continually, momentary gestures and phrases of Alex's invaded her thoughts. His dancing eyes flirted with her reflection in the mirror as she swept her hair up into a bouquet of curls.

Jarred knocked on Nikki's door. Nikki's going out again with a man she had met only that afternoon disturbed him. He plied her with questions, none of which she could answer. Since Nikki refused to ice her plans and dismissed the need for his security services that evening, Jarred departed an unhappy person.

At eight, Nikki rode the elevator down to the second floor. She decided she'd descend the grand staircase to make an entrance. A cursory scan of the lobby, from atop the stairs, didn't turn up anyone who remotely resembled Alexander. As she began her descent, a tuxedo-attired gentleman stepped from the staircase's shadows and slowly turned toward her. There stood the appraising Mr. Vincente.

Alexander drank her in, lapping up every nuance, every step of her grand entrance. Extending his hand, he took her gloved hand to assist her down the last two steps.

From behind his back, he produced a single flower nosegay. With a twinkle in his eyes, he said, "I understand you like gardenias."

Utter surprise flashed across her face. Instantly, she understood. "You! All these months! It's been you!"

His impish blues danced. "I think they fit your style—delicate elegance and sophistication in a simple package. Shall we go?" With his hand lightly on her back, he guided her to his waiting limousine.

Getting into the car, a few pops and blinding flashes greeted them. Nothing unusual—just the tabloid photographers catching Nikki in the company of someone new. Nikki apologized once they settled into their seats. "That's a hazard of my profession. In truth, I'm surprised they didn't nail us while we were shopping."

They dined at an intimate restaurant called the Pearl, nestled into Hong Kong's Causeway Bay. The staff referred to Alexander by name and seated them at the best table by the window. The busy causeway provided a kaleidoscope of the seaport cosmos as the little junks migrated back and forth over the water. Their winking lanterns resembled diamonds twinkling against the velvet backdrop of night. They supped slowly, first champagne, then oysters, followed by seafood bisque. Engaging banter accompanied each course.

Conversation flowed easily with Alex. He steered the topic back to their shopping earlier in the day. "This afternoon when you recognized Charlie Soo for his integrity and value of friendship, you paid him the highest compliment possible. Charlie is a hard-bitten businessman who scratched his way up from those back alleys of Hong Kong which you find so charming. He doesn't give anything away and doesn't make friends easily."

"I was honored by the offer of his friendship. How long have you known him?"

"Fifteen years. We've been in some tight spots together. I've trusted him with my life many times."

Alex's admission of tight spots surprised Nikki and served to point up how much she didn't know about him. Over the Cantonese lobster curry, she commented, "Trusted friends are indeed a rarity. But I must admit I can't imagine you being caught off guard by anything, let alone being in a 'tight spot.'"

Alex cautiously smiled across the lip of his wineglass. "That's in the past. I'd rather deal with the present. Your *savoir faire* fascinates me. I find your uncanny ability to relate to people refreshing."

Despite the compliment, his move to redirect her attention caught an edge with her. Resting her fork on her plate, Nikki asked, "How long have you been watching me anyway? The first time I recall seeing you was in Naples on my eighteenth birthday."

Holding his wineglass, Alexander relaxed into the back of his chair. "It was spring of 1965 in the Brass Rail Café, not far from the Circus in London. You met a reporter there. I didn't catch much, but I remember you totally disarmed him. He wound up practically groveling at your feet. He called you Princess—so fitting!"

Nikki searched her memory. "You mean Karl?"

"Okay, Karl… You fascinated me the moment you walked in the door. I would have introduced myself then, but you left with the guy. Before long, 'Nikki' began to pop up all over the place. I followed your career in the press. Naples was your first concert I caught. You enchanted me."

"Heavens, Alex, that was almost two years ago. I remember you kept showing up—at the premiere party, then outside the farm in Pennsylvania. That scared me."

"Understandable, but I needed to make sure you were all right," he ceded apologetically.

The uneasiness from the encounter on the farm filtered into Nikki's memory. *Was this man just a charming eccentric? A celebrity stalker? A con artist? What?* Suddenly feeling ill at ease, she wished she had taken Jarred's protestations to heart.

Alexander read her fear. Honestly smiling, he leaned forward. "You see, Nicole, since that day in the café, I have been totally captivated by your charm. Not by Nikki, but by you. In fact, your public persona only complicated the possibility of an introduction."

Nikki weakly smiled.

Dismayed, Alex sat back. "I am terribly sorry. I have frightened you. That was never my intent. If you like, I will call in your security team, and they can take you back to your hotel." He readied his hand to motion.

Nikki arrested his signal. "Security?" *If only they were there*, she wished.

Placating her, Alex smiled. "You don't think your head of security would let you out with a stranger at night without sending someone along to keep an eye on him, do you?"

"Jarred stopped by earlier in the evening, and I dismissed him. You must be paranoid if you think we're being followed." Nikki laughed accusingly.

The possibility of a challenge excited Alex; he smiled, raising his glass. "Princess, how much would you like to bet?"

Cocksure of herself, she met his challenge. "Name your poison," she dared him with her raised glass. She knew Jarred and his regard for orders.

"If security is present, then you will know you are in good hands, and we shall continue our date in their presence. If no one is there, then you will immediately call Jarred to come and rescue you. And I promise I will never show up on your doorstep or bother you again. Deal?" His glass waited for hers to commence the bet.

In the exhilaration of the moment, Nikki picked up the gauntlet Alex tossed down. "Deal." She clinked his glass.

Alexander tapped his chin in thought. "Now how to prove this?"

"We could always go out into the street. You would hold my arm, and I'd call for help," Nikki volunteered.

"Great plan! And risk getting shot?" Alex chortled at the absurdity.

"Shot? Guns? Oooh, Mr. Vincente, you watch too many movies."

"My dear, how green are you?" Their game of wits electrified him. "You do not think your security is defenseless, do you? I am not about to risk my hide on your naiveté. No, there has to be another way."

"Then I'll go out by myself and call for help. When no one comes, I'll come back into the restaurant and call Jarred."

"I'm not sure I like it. This smacks of crying wolf. But if done well, it should be rather effective. Please do me a slight favor. Warn the maître d' before you pull off this thing. We do not want the police showing up too."

The moment of truth had arrived. Nikki gathered her things. Once she walked out, she didn't plan on coming back. She knew she was right; Jarred wouldn't dare trespass on her privacy against her order. Yet Nikki felt a twinge that maybe she had carried this bet thing a bit too far. She didn't really want the evening to end, especially in an absurd challenge of egos. She wanted to get to know this gentleman. But she had painted herself into a corner, so her feelings constituted water under the bridge now.

Alex stood up when she rose to leave. "If you are right, you realize this is goodbye," he lamented with a sigh. "I want you to know this has been the most marvelous night of my life, for which I do sincerely thank you. I will treasure it always. May I, one last time?" He reached for her hand.

Raising her hand to his lips, he simulated a slight snap to attention, then he clicked his heels. "Goodbye, my dear Nicole. Thank you again." He kissed her hand and, as a gentleman, maintained his standing position until she left the room.

Nikki didn't turn around lest she give him quarter or grant herself a chance to renege on their wager. Drawing up to her full height, she walked out proudly. Nikki was sure as soon as she left, he blithely returned to his seat to plan his next conquest of some other unsuspecting damsel in the city.

In keeping with her promise, she stopped by the maître d's stand and briefly explained the wager. Not wishing to impugn the reputation of the fine establishment, Nikki walked to midblock before beginning her call for help.

Almost from the moment her foot stepped out of range of the building's light into the darkness of the deserted sidewalk, Nikki heard a slight scuffling. Memories of Buenos Aires poured over her. She froze. Her mind launched into hyperdrive. *What if I'm right and there is no security out here? Oh, those footsteps! What have I set myself up for? The maître d' will assume my cries are just the bet.* Panic reared its head. Summoning anything that remotely resembled courage, Nikki shook off the fear, determined to carry out the silly wager.

She raised her voice into the night air. "Help! Oh please someone help me!" It didn't take but a second—the footfalls came fast and furious. Almost instantly, two figures flashed from the shadows and rushed at her. In the ambient light from the street, to her relief, Nikki saw it was Edward, and Jarred himself, flying to her side brandishing firearms. Her jaw dropped visibly. With genuine contriteness, Nikki profusely apologized for her careless disregard of their jobs.

To her surprise, Jarred dismissed her attempts at repentance while holstering his weapon. He regretted his covert actions and not disclosing his presence to her.

Turning around to go back to the restaurant and eat her double serving of crow, to her amazement, Alex waited, leaning one elbow up against his limousine, smiling.

"You win!" Nikki admitted, throwing up her hands. Then she introduced Jarred and Edward.

Pulling himself up for the introductions, Alexander warmly greeted them, "Gentlemen, I do sincerely apologize for sending you on this little exercise. I am afraid I put her up to this. Please feel welcome to accompany us for the rest of the evening. See, I have a cab waiting so you can follow along."

He turned to her. "I thought we might catch dessert somewhere else." Once inside the car, Alex addressed her earnestly. "Nicole, if you are not comfortable with me, I will release you from the wager and take you back to the hotel. I would never do anything to make you ill at ease. What is your pleasure?" Then he added with a hopeful twinkle in his eyes, "Or shall we continue?"

"Yes. I'm fine. Please." Nikki studied his suave self-assurance for a moment. "How long were you standing there?"

"For pretty much all of it. I couldn't let you walk out into the night alone. What if you had been right? Who would have been there to protect you?"

"How did you know they would be there?"

"It was really—as you say—a sure thing. I know that if I had such a precious jewel to protect, I would never let it out of my sight. Like all good security, they are devoted to their mission."

"And the guns?"

"It's just part of the job, especially after Buenos Aires. Jarred knows the business and his subject. He knew a gun would frighten you. There was really no need for you to know."

"You know about Buenos Aires?"

"Nicole, I told you that I have been interested in you since that day in the café. You are important to me. I travel a lot in my job. Our paths intersected when I could arrange it."

"Then you knew I was married."

"I discovered that after the premiere. I did not show up after that."

"Except for the farm incident."

"After the roughing up Grant gave you, I figured he must be out of your life. Besides, I was concerned."

"Grant? How could you have known about that?"

"I have connections." Alexander wrapped his hands around both of hers. "But that is all in the past. Please just take it that I cared and let us not drag up all the details. I want you to be at ease with me. Do you still feel comfortable here?"

"Yes. It's just that I'm stunned at how much you know. It's a little disconcerting." Then a thought struck her. "You know, for such a sucker's bet, that was some farewell scene you put on back there at the restaurant."

Devilish amusement again sparkled in his eyes. He picked up her gloved hand, raised it to his lips, and, with a cock of his head and a glint in his eyes, said, *"Carpe diem!"*

The limo drew to a stop in front of the Furama Hotel. "I thought some dessert and coffee in the dining room at the top of the hotel. Next to you, it is the best view in town."

Alexander was right. The Furama offered a magnificent view of the entire harbor. They finished their decadent chocolate torte and relaxed over espressos as the entire seaport revolved below them. Alex brought out the little satin sac from Mr. Soo's shop. "See what you think of this. I had it done this afternoon." He opened the sac to reveal an exquisite setting. A triangular cluster of three small diamonds gathered around the top point of the pear shape to perfectly accent the ruby.

"Oh, Alexander, it's elegant! You do have good taste."

"May I put it on you?" As Alex leaned in to her, his masculine fragrance filled her nose.

Opening the clasp, he gently placed it around her neck, letting the pendant come to rest perfectly on her breastbone, tantalizingly above her cleavage. "Beautiful," he whispered admiringly.

"Oh, it is. Thank you."

"I wasn't speaking about the jewelry." Alexander fixed his eyes intently on her.

The directness of his compliment caught Nikki's breath. Unable to respond, she changed the subject. "You must let me know what I owe you for it."

"I thought we agreed this afternoon that I would get the setting."

"I only meant you could select one. I never presumed you'd buy it."

"Nicole, it is an innocent bauble. Think of it as a souvenir from our day together."

Brandies with Alex quieted any further discussion of the matter. The nightcaps and conversation carried them to three in the morning, when they climbed back into the limo for the ride back to Nikki's hotel.

Parked in front of the hotel, they had trouble bringing the evening to an end. "May I see you again today?" Alex asked.

"I wish I could," Nikki fumbled. "We leave in the late afternoon. I have a thousand things to do before the plane, including my final chat session at three."

"What about breakfast?"

"Like in four or five more hours?" Nikki looked at her watch.

Alex walked her to the elevator. "Why not take care of your obligations, and I will see you at seven for breakfast."

Not really wanting their date to end, Nikki capitulated. "Okay, seven it is."

With a hand kiss, Alexander sent her up to her hotel suite.

Nikki tried to organize herself for departure, but the evening crept into every deliberation. Visions of Alexander's tanned physique, so elegantly accentuated in his crisp formal wear, usurped all other thoughts. She took the necklace off and displayed it so she could delight in it. Then she put it back on, to have him near her. Emptying her closet to sort out her short-trip bag to go home, again she revisited how the candlelight kissed the gold from his hair and smoldered in his eyes, those indelible blue eyes.

What time is it?

At six-thirty, she woke Mary. "Mary, I'm really sorry, but this time I'm going to dump all the prep for leaving on you. Something's come up, and I made plans for this morning and afternoon."

Finally able to focus, her friend's gaze fell with incriminating curiosity on the green silk dress that she still had on. "I guess you do have plans! What's going on? What about the chat session? Do you want me to cancel that?"

"No. I wouldn't miss it for the world. I've got to change now. I met someone. I'll be at the chat session in the hotel conference room at three." On her way out, she stopped. "You're really a friend. Thanks so very much."

Never once in their over two years together had Nikki ever presumed or trespassed on her best friend. So Mary knew this had to be something really big.

In anticipation of a time crunch at the end, Nicole settled on the typical Nikki dress for the day: a black-and-white houndstooth miniskirt, an electric yellow poet's blouse, and matching tights. It wasn't how she wanted to meet Alexander, but she doubted she'd have time to change before the chat session. Not wanting to give up the ruby pendant, she slipped it underneath her blouse and threw on a strand of "kicky" white plastic beads with matching hoop earrings, then tossed makeup in her purse for touch-ups.

The doors to the elevator opened to the lobby shortly after seven. Alexander waited with the *Asian Wall Street Journal* tucked beneath his arm. He appeared fresh and dashing in a blue-and-white pin-striped oxford shirt, gray slacks, and a navy blazer. He greeted her with a European-style peck to the cheek and a smile. "I hoped you would keep our date. It was rather rude of me to suggest you give up your sleep to spend some time with me."

"And who's to say I didn't catch a few winks?" Nikki jibed. She didn't want him to think she had actually dropped everything for him.

Catching a double-decker, they rode uptown to the Prestige de Ville. "They have the best Eggs Benedict this side of Brennan's in New Orleans," Alex extolled. Over breakfast, he commented on her attire, "My, you do look incredibly 'Nikki' today."

"I know. But since I'll be 'on' this afternoon, I had to dress the part."

"And speaking of the day, what did you have on the agenda for us today?" he asked with great interest.

"Alex, you asked me. I thought you had something in mind."

"I only wanted to be in the presence of your company. The day is yours. Seize it. I am but your humble servant."

"Okay, Christmas is less than a week away. I really planned to do some shopping for gifts yesterday, but I kind of got sidetracked." She shot him a coy smile.

Finishing breakfast, they headed to the ferry for the shopping mecca of Kowloon.

Shopping with Alexander wasn't like crawling through the boutiques on Carnaby Street with Candy or even browsing at stuffy Harrods with Mary. No, Alexander elevated shopping to an aristocratic art form. They shopped from atop gilt chairs of silk brocade, with their feet propped up on little footstools, sipping jasmine-infused tea, while attentive staff paraded and demonstrated their wares before them. At one boutique, the selection of pearl-beaded angora sweaters so delighted Nikki, she bought not only one for her mom, but also a couple for herself too. On their way out of the shop, she stopped to admire a pale-blue silk business suit with pearl buttons.

"It would be exquisite on you," Alex encouraged.

"I know." Nikki sighed a lament. "But when would I wear it? It's not 'Nikki.'"

"Surely, Nicole Moore ventures out every now and again."

"Maybe, sometime." She half-considered it as she continued toward the exit.

Alex nodded.

They swam their way through the people-choked sidewalks from one shopping tower to the next when Alex abruptly stopped. A tilt of his head drew Nikki's attention to the merchandise in the store window. Sleek feminine forms displayed an eclectic array of high-fashion lingerie—bras, panties, filmy peignoirs.

"Shall we?" Alex dared with a saucy wink.

Embarrassed, but not about to display it for him, Nikki burst out laughing and kept walking.

Their arms would have been full from shopping, but Alex hired runners to periodically dispatch the treasures back to the hotel.

Occasionally, someone on the street recognized Nikki and stopped her for an autograph or a picture. Over lunch, she apologized after one rather drawn-out encounter.

Alex stopped her midsentence. "This is not something new that you just invented. It is your job. Besides," he teased, "better you working than me."

His reference to their meeting the day before afforded Nikki another opportunity to delve into his pursuit of her. "Yesterday, when you stepped into the Kwan scam, your presence there, at that precise moment, didn't just happen by accident, did it?"

Straightforwardly, Alex answered, "No."

"How long were you following me?"

"Nicole"—he temporarily shelved his natural amusement—"I would not call it following you. When I discovered that my business trip coincided with your tour, I made sure that our paths crossed. I just had to wait for the right opportunity for my introduction to present itself."

Nikki laughed. "Thank goodness for the Kwan brothers, huh?"

He returned the smile. "I am sorry it took so long for them to appear on the scene. If they had been more on target, I wouldn't be fighting for precious minutes of your time at the end of your visit. Perhaps I should put them on my payroll."

"Speaking of payroll, Alex, what exactly do you do?"

As if he totally missed her question, he asked, "What are you doing for New Year's Eve?"

"Why? I don't know. Probably spending it on the farm with my parents before heading back to London."

"Spend it here with me. The city really celebrates—fireworks, parades, dancing in the streets," he pushed to make the spontaneous sale.

"You mean come back here in two weeks?" Nikki cringed at the thought of another eighteen-hour flight.

"No. Don't go home today. Stay! Have Christmas here with me. Then we will do New Year's!"

"But I promised my parents I'd be home for Christmas."

Alex interrupted, "Bring them here. We can celebrate together in Hong Kong. It's not snow and sleigh rides, but then again, is Pennsylvania really? It will be different, and I promise I will make it exciting!"

Nikki didn't doubt that. More than anything, she wanted to throw caution to the wind and jump on the idea. But she didn't want to have her parents rearrange their plans again, not to mention on the whim of someone she had just met—talk about irresponsibility!

As the minutes ticked away on the clock, Nikki grew anxious. She wished the afternoon would stretch on for an eternity, but her commitment to the fans followed by her immediate departure pressed in on her. She didn't even need to ask. Almost before she thought it, Alex whisked her back to the hotel in plenty of time. Alexander consented to staying for the chat session, taking a chair in the far rear. As the session drew to a close, her eyes sought out Alex. At some point, he must have quietly slipped out. Nikki had hoped for a goodbye; obviously he didn't do them. Or maybe in declining his invitation to stay, she had trampled on his ego.

The customary manila envelope already occupied Nikki's seat in the first-class section of the aircraft, no doubt housing the usual details of last-minute items. However, instead of itinerary changes, this one contained several eight-by-ten glossies of Alex and her from their date. Nikki tarried over the sweetness of the memory as Karl slid into the vacant seat next to her.

"Know who he is?" Karl asked sardonically while tightening his seat belt.

Taken aback by the tonal inference of his question, uncharacteristically she bristled. "You intend on staying? Yes, that's Alexander Vincente... Why? Do you know where these came from?"

"Yeah, Jimmy took them last night when the two of you stepped out."

"Karl, are you spying on me? I thought we were friends?" she accused.

"Calm down, Nikki. We are friends. I wasn't spying either. I figured I had better get those first rather than someone else. We've always worked like that... Wow, are we a bit touchy today!"

"I'm sorry. I'm a little tired. I didn't get any sleep last night," she confessed.

"I'm not casting aspersions. But what do you know about this guy?" Karl asked, still actively concerned.

"I apologize. You hit a nerve. I'm a little angry with myself because in truth, I don't know too much about him." Nikki tossed the photos back into the envelope. "I realize it's stupid. I'm already beating myself up over that. On the other hand, Karl, I find him... interesting... All I know is that he was in the Brass Rail Café the day you and I first hammered out our publicity deal. He's had a thing for me ever since."

"What happened to your hard and fast rule to never date anyone outside the show business world?" Karl questioned.

"Alex's circles of influence crush the entertainment world. I get the distinct impression that our 'world' rather repulses him. Besides, he travels a lot and he showed up in Hong Kong to introduce himself. I tried to find out what exactly he does, but he avoided the question. With the hectic pace of the day though, I don't know if it was intentional or if it slipped through the cracks."

"My guess would be intentional." Karl pulled the photos back out of the envelope. "That's Alexander Vincente, international playboy. A *bon vivant* employed by whatever breeze is blowing today."

Then Karl produced another envelope with several grainy black-and-white candid photos, apparently taken covertly, of Alex shot at various world locales, some with shapely women on his arm. "I had my editor telex me these this afternoon. I wanted to be sure I was right."

The plane started to roll down the runway.

"Karl, the last time I looked, it wasn't a crime to be rich, good-looking, or at your leisure."

"Wouldn't we all like to be? But there have been some questionable occurrences surrounding him." Determined, Karl refused to drop the topic.

"Such as?"

"Sometimes things turn up missing: rare antiquities, priceless masterpieces, valuable jewels, money, and people have disappeared."

"You have got to be kidding!" Incredulity crept into Nikki's voice. "Doesn't that smack a lot of spy hooey to you?"

The plane lifted off. The seaport with Alexander Vincente in it shrank, then disappeared.

"When did you put this all together?" Nikki returned her attention to her friend.

"Not until Jimmy showed me the pictures this morning. I admit most of what I told you reeks of rumor and innuendo."

"Does Jarred know? Shouldn't I be hearing this from him?" Nikki tried to shove the bird-dogging off onto someone else, figuring if Jarred had concerns, he would have already done some investigating of his own.

Karl continued, "I gave it to him as soon as I got confirmation on the pictures. I'd tread lightly with Jarred if I were you. He's a bit sensitive over last night. You know the two of you scared the hell out of him."

"I know. I apologized. But I'll talk to him again."

"I'll leave you alone for now, Nikki. Just be careful, okay? I know I don't have a right. It's just that I don't want to see you hurt." Karl unbuckled his seat belt to make his exit, leaving the envelope with the black and whites behind.

Finishing off dinner with a tad more wine, Nikki watched the sky transform itself into night. The twinkling stars reminded her of

Alexander's eyes and their night at the Pearl. Karl's ominous warnings didn't faze her. The description of a playboy squared perfectly with the polished manners accompanied by Alex's devil-may-care attitude. Nikki wondered if she'd see him again. As much as she hoped for another rendezvous, she expected nothing. After all, she had turned him down. She suspected men like him were accustomed to having their own way. With plenty of fish in the sea, Nikki assumed he was already angling for the next flounder, so she wrote off Mr. Vincente.

Homey family traditions swirling with the aromas of cinnamon, pine, and bayberry ushered in Christmas in Pennsylvania. The Moores' celebration deliberately lacked the showbiz glitz that so inundated the house just a month before for her TV special. Mom loved her sweater, and Dad tinkered all day with the superminiaturized radio Nikki gave him.

A messenger arrived just before dinner with a package for Nikki. She unwrapped the blue silk suit she had admired in Hong Kong. The card simply read, "For Nicole Moore—Merry Christmas." Nikki knew immediately who sent it. But since the card wasn't signed, for her parents' benefit, she speculated about who on her staff might have been so generous.

On New Year's Eve, Cookie, Annie, and Leanne swung by. Realizing it could be the last time the four of them might be together unencumbered by partners, they spent a quiet evening at Nikki's parents' house. Their plans included only a fierce game of Monopoly and ordering cheesesteaks from V&S. At eleven, Nikki answered the knock at the front door. It wasn't the sandwiches, but a delivery of another sort.

Beneath all the special packaging, the box contained a bottle of Cristal champagne and a card: "I'm watching the fireworks explode over Hong Kong harbor, missing you. Share a drink with me at midnight. Here's to 1967! Alexander."

To say the least, the delivery enlivened the house. Since Nikki hadn't mentioned Alex to anyone, now there were questions to be answered. Nikki's mom, dad, and the three girls grilled her. Pulling the ruby pendant out from underneath her sweater, Nikki started with the Kwan brothers, although she deliberately omitted Karl's vague allegations.

Later on New Year's Day, her father borrowed the pendant to put it under his scope. Nikki watched as he maneuvered the piece under the instrument. "Nikki, your gentleman friend really knows his business. The diamonds he had set for you aren't throwaways. They may be small, but they are blue-white, flawless. Normally you would never set such stones as accent pieces. I would say the diamonds outvalue the center stone except… How much did you say you paid for the ruby?"

"Seven hundred dollars. Why?" she asked. Knowing even what little she did about Alex, her father's appraisal didn't shock her.

"You stole it! If I bought it *wholesale*, I'd have paid at least seven thousand for it. Rarely have I seen a ruby of such quality. Make sure you insure it well." However, this bit of news, while delighting her, also angered Nikki.

She fumed as she made her way from her father's home office to the kitchen. *Obviously Mr. Vincente planned to make a fool of me! The diamonds he had set, the value of the ruby, the deal for the stone I supposedly made with Charlie Soo…all of it as arranged by Alexander Vincente! He knew all along. He engineered it all! So it wasn't mere coincidence that the ruby's price exactly matched the price of the Kwan fake! Did he play me for a reaction to further amuse himself? Was it a test? A game?* Nikki resolved, *The next time he swaggers into my life for a meeting, he will hear from me. And of course, after the suit and the champagne, I know there will be another encounter.*

Nikki's tussle of thoughts followed her to the kitchen where she tried to settle herself on a chair at the kitchen table. *To be sure, Alexander Vincente presents a significant challenge of wits. And I will not be bested by his smug air of aristocracy.* Idealistically, she steeled herself for their next go-around, never realizing he epitomized both her salvation and quicksand.

In contemplating the timing of her next face-off with Mr. Vincente, Nikki's mind wandered to the actual timing of that meeting amid the frenetic schedule posed by her solo singing career. *To maintain the sensation of a lightning wild career, no doubt Bruce has lined out plenty of studio time, chats, TV, and tours across half the known world for me! I will have to hustle to keep up with his fast-paced schedule.* Nikki sniffed a laugh. *Maybe Alexander Vincente will have to wrestle a few things to catch up with me!*

Thoughts of timing and schedules veered Nikki's reverie onto the Agency. In her young and still terribly naïve life experience, so far Nikki only saw the Agency as a patriotic ticket to excitement rather than realizing it promised poisonous consequences. With each contact from Junger and Mann, the Agency's fangs insinuated themselves deeper into her very core, extracting life and injecting lethal venom.

Abruptly, an insistent rap at the front door disrupted her thoughts. Not hearing either of her parents making their way to the door, Nikki resigned to answer it.

She swung the solid panel door open. A rush of winter wind stung her. There stood a stranger in a black top coat, wearing a dark suit, tie, and starched white shirt. A pair of dark aviator glasses hid his soul.

"Hello, Miss Moore," he declared.

"May I help you?" His foreknowledge and bluntness stunned her.

"I'm from the Agency." In a blur, he flashed credentials and a badge. "This is for you." Boldly, he produced then handed her an envelope.

"What? Why?" Questions tumbled out of Nikki all at once. "Who exactly are you? I hardly saw the Agency's logo, let alone your name. What do you want with me?"

"The envelope..." With frustration, he gestured toward the plain white cover.

At his insistence, Nikki sliced the sealed envelope opened with her index finger. She read the four words on the enclosed sheet of paper:

Tomorrow, my office.

—Mann

Puzzled she eyed the messenger.

"I'm here to assist you. We need to go now!" he stressed.
Nikki read the note again asking with incredulity, "That's it?"
The man asserted, "That, and so much *more!*"

ACKNOWLEDGMENTS

To Jerry Lee Rothermel whose love and confidence in my abilities saw me through the tough times, I thank you for backing me in all those important ways.

Thank you to Rita Cobain Brown, the toughest editor and best friend a book ever had. Without her focus, this book would not have been possible. My friend always.

To Lynette Good, for her assistance over the years with editing and helping me sort out ideas, especially those that demanded spur-of-the-moment timing. You are appreciated.

Thank you also to the many that have had profound influence:

My mother and father, Mary Frances and Richard Rairigh, for their wisdom and guidance.

My daughters, Kristina, Victoria, Jodi, and Jacki, for their support.

Dr. Herbert W. Robinson who helped me refine my writing ability with the valuable editing experience of his two books.

To my mentor, Fay Gridley, who supported me in life and through this process.

My teachers, June McKnight, Michael Rasmussen, Robert Arner, and Harry Hude, who made significant contributions to the fundamentals of my writing and fer larnin' me good.

And to John for providing the impetus and inspiration.

ABOUT THE AUTHOR

"I have always seen the world in words," remarks Tammie in an interview. "It's never just snowing. It's 'thick, goose-size feathers of snow filled up the landscape.'"

In grade school, Tammie wrote little dramas for her classmates to act out during recess. At North Farmington High, she wrote two books on life in a hot rock group. Central Michigan University further honed her writing skills. Later, her writing ability and community involvement through the Chamber of Commerce garnered her a spot in the Fountain Hills Hall of Fame.

Tammie; her husband, Jerry; and their four daughters with their families have been Arizona residents for the last forty-five years.